BEDFORD AVENUE

Incidents in a Small Town

Kristopher Schultz

Bedford Avenue, Incidents in a Small Town is a work of fiction. Names, characters, places, and incidents are the products of the author's imagination or are used fictitiously. Any resemblance to actual events, locales, or persons, living or dead, is entirely coincidental (except for John and Debbi at the Old Town Grill who make the best burgers in town).

Although despite this disclaimer, everyone who reads these stories seems to think they are reading about their own family and friends.

Which I think is good.

Cover Photograph: Kristopher Schultz

Author Photograph: Melinda Gray

Published by Create Space Independent Publishing Platform

ISBN-13:978-1490350189

ISBN-10:1490350187

www.facebook.com/kristopherschultzauthor

www.kristopherschultz.com

"Get your facts first, then you can distort them as you please."

-Mark Twain

"In small towns people scent the wind with noses of uncommon keenness."

-Stephen King

For my ladies...

Joslin, Reily, and Sooz

xo

BEDFORD AVENUE

Incidents in a Small Town

Kristopher Schultz

Acknowledgements

Any story worth telling needs an editor to ensure the tale is worth reading. Thank you to my editor, Jill Kramer, for catching my errors and telling me where I was wrong. Although, since my editor is also my mother, she would probably like to thank me for giving her the opportunity to correct her son. You're welcome mom.

Hello and thank you to my oncologist Dr. Tsai and his wonderful staff. Your work has allowed me to write these stories and enjoy a great life.

Thank you to my friends and family for leading such rich lives.

And finally, thank you to my first and favorite reader, my spouse, Sooz. Your smile and laugh are what I look forward to every day (though I do enjoy the foot rubs too).

K.S.

TABLE OF CONTENTS

Introduction

Dearest family, friends, and foothill residents,

Moving here some twenty-five years ago was a most fortunate accident. Sooz and I were young, broke, fresh out of college in Santa Barbara, and hoping to move to the green promise land of Oregon to begin our lives together. But the mid-1980's were a tough time for teachers up north, so we looked for a growing area in northern California that would welcome two enthusiastic educators.

At first, to be honest, the culture shock was difficult to accept. Though neither of us had ever been to Kansas, we both felt as if we were suffering from a reverse "Dorothy Syndrome" in which we had left Oz and been dropped into a pair of wooden rockers on Auntie Em's front porch.

To say life moves slower here in the foothills is a compliment and a choice. The grocery clerks ask me about my kids, and the guy behind the plumbing counter actually fixes my bathroom faucet himself, all while he is telling me that I can do the repair myself.

My neighbors are friendly, polite, and always have a story to share. They will gladly bring in the mail and feed the cats when asked. And not a one of them complained when my two teenage daughters were learning to drive.

Colleagues and coworkers at school continue to astound me with their kindness, generosity, and professionalism. They do anything and everything for students while supporting each of them to reach his or her potential as an individual. Teachers are indispensable. And every last one of them has a story about a deer hitting their car.

The foothills of the Sierra Nevada Mountains are beautiful, but the people of this area are what makes this region such a great place to live. Gold was first discovered not far from here in 1848 and the world rushed in to claim a share. Plenty of treasure is still here in town, you just need to slow down and talk with folks so the riches don't pass you by.

So when reading the incidents that follow, if you come across a character or an event and think, "Hey, he's talking about me!" let me be clear: If you find the portrayal to be complimentary, flattering, or you find yourself thoroughly entertained, then yes, you were undoubtably the inspiration, and thank you very much. However, if you find the characterization shocking, offensive, or a betrayal of friendship, then no, you were definitely not the inspiration, a horrible misunderstanding has occurred, and thank you very much.

-Kristopher Schultz

Placerville, California

CHAPTER ONE

The Fourth of July Parade is on the Fourth of July

Ask local curmudgeon Maxine Baxter about the prettiest parade in the country and the eighty-five-year-old gardener with the most fragrant flower garden in town will tell you about the Tournament of Roses Parade in Pasadena. The annual New Year's Day event is loaded with flowers, petals, and seeds so it even smells like a wonderful parade. But if you ask Maxine about the best parade in the country, she won't mention Pasadena. She'll tell you about our Fourth of July parade that rolls through Main Street each year.

Due to all the horses our parade may not smell like roses, but the event offers something for everyone and the day is certainly one of the social highlights of the year. The parade is a gathering of people that celebrates both our past and our present. And every year the occasion brings Maxine, escorted by her ninety-four-year-old husband Clarence, down to the Bell Tower to shed her grumpiness and enjoy the pomp and faire of the world's best parade. There's no point in arguing with Maxine or trying to convince her on the merits of some other parade because Maxine is always right. If you don't believe her, just ask and she'll set you straight.

Leading off this year's festivities was City Councilman, insurance salesman, and proud grandfather Carl Snyder along with his three granddaughters. Carl rigged up a pair of bullhorn speakers on the roof of his Ford station wagon blasting out "Stars and Stripes Forever" as he drove behind his three baton-twirling granddaughters. The seven, eight, and ten-year-old ladies each wearing a homemade red, white, and blue dance outfit marched down the middle of Main Street following the double-yellow line to the cheers of an appreciative crowd lining both sides of the street.

Those who weren't already standing now rose as the Boy Scouts marched past carrying several United States flags. Mayor, pack leader, and proud grandfather Carl Romano saluted the crowd as he marched with his two grandsons. There had been some debate on the City Council as to who should be the first parade entry this year, Carl's grandsons with their flags or the other Carl's granddaughters with their batons. Eventually the two Councilmen agreed to alternate the honor which seemed an unusually reasonable solution for our local government. The decision was probably aided by the fact that no one else on the council had grandkids that were old enough yet to march in the parade.

The Folding Lawn Chair Brigade and Precision Drill Team came next, who this year were without the participation of Walt Peterson. Walt was sidelined after an unfortunate accident during practice left him with both a sprained ankle and wrist. Walt had difficulty with the "pivot, unfold, sit" maneuver when his "unfold" was not completed before he proceeded to "sit." Walt and his wife Barb took in the parade on one of the benches beneath the Bell Tower. Team trainer and local dentist Dr. Gary reports that Walt will be fully recovered for next year's parade.

Rob and Jennifer Taylor brought Jen's grandmother Mary Thorpe to the parade. Mary's eyesight doesn't allow her to see much at a distance, but she loved the high school band performing "It's a Grand Old Flag." Although she did keep asking why the marching musicians were dressed as giant Q-tips.

As a collection of Model T and Model A cars drove by, Jen described the vehicles to Mary hoping to elicit a story or two, but

Mary was more interested in chatting with the young De Luca family she just met. Tino and Lisa, along with their boys Michael and Rocco, were new arrivals to town and this was their first parade. Mary encouraged the boys to be ready for the fire trucks that would come along toward the end of the parade. Mary was also taken with Tino's shiny hat, as she was a collector herself. She had a good laugh at herself after Tino explained he wasn't wearing a hat, he was just bald and it was a warm, sunny day.

Local landscaping genius Samantha Thompson sponsored the first float in the parade. Sam unloaded her backhoe off the trailer and hitched the trailer to the back of her diesel pickup. Members of Friends of the Animal Shelter rode in the truck bed, while members of the Garden Club rode on the trailer. The animal lovers got the better deal as the flower lovers spent more time holding on to the trailer than smiling and waving to the crowd. With the bouncing ride and diesel fumes proving to be too much, the Garden Club spent the second half of the parade walking in front of Sam's truck.

A flatbed truck holding local Republicans was supposed to be separated from a flatbed truck holding local Democrats, but the third-grade class of Mr. Barry Reese wasn't ready at the start of the parade so our local political groups had to be on their best behavior. A few heated debates ensued between the two vehicles until they reached the Bell Tower. That's when Maxine Baxter stepped out of the crowd and gave both groups what for, barking at them and not so politely ordering them to put some distance between themselves. Nobody argued with Maxine because Maxine was right.

Apparently Mr. Reese had forgotten the scheduled assembly time to meet in the grocery store parking lot at the other end of town. At least that explanation was better than the other reason floating around. He forgot the date of the parade. Mr. Reese and his class did make the parade, but had the unfortunate placement of following the Appaloosa enthusiasts. Of course the kids were preceded by the traditional Pooper Scooper Groupers that were instituted to follow all live animal parade entrants after the unfortunate incident involving the Mounted Posse Search and Rescue Team and the high school band several years ago, but the third graders were still seen side stepping and nose holding their way down Main Street. Despite the unusual marching technique, the crowd still appreciated the "Remember to Reduce, Reuse, and Recycle" message promoted by the students with their signs and matching tye-dye t-shirts.

A line of convertibles donated for the day by downtown's one auto dealer carried various local city officials. City Council members Charlie Tuttle and Deborah Singerman each rode solo in their drop tops with Foothill Motors banners hanging on the side of each car. Councilman Dr. Marcus Gilbert's banners had been covered with a pair of white sheets and some hastily made signs, Gilbert Chiropractic, along with his phone number.

The Chief of Police, Captain of the Fire Department, and Miss Fourth of July each got their own convertible too. Four other folks nobody in the crowd seemed to know also got individual convertible rides. These mystery guests generated enough conversation around town you can be sure the City Council will discuss and implement a new official procedure for determining who gets a convertible for next year's parade.

A bunch of rowdy, unshaven guys in red shirts and blue jeans came through on the back of an empty logging truck. Every one of them had a beer in his hand and looked like he had already emptied quite a few more before the parade. Parade watchers couldn't be sure if the boys were loaded or just playing the part, but they certainly were a happy bunch. John Forrester explained they were Clampers. Members of E Clampus Vitus, a fraternal organization that says they're either a drinking group that likes history or a historical group that likes to drink. These boys are dedicated to the preservation of overlooked historic sites of the Gold Rush era, like an old mine, a unique saloon, or a friendly brothel. They often insist on throwing a substantial party after placing a ceremonial monument or plaque at a site. Some say they are a darn good service group, though the only evidence of them providing any service today was the trailer they were pulling which contained two functioning outhouses.

Following these gentlemen came two fire trucks. The first one, an antique hook and ladder truck, was loaded with volunteer firefighters. Men and women with big smiles on their faces and tired arms from throwing candy to the crowd the entire length of the parade. Michael and Rocco De Luca looked to mom and didn't need to be told twice. They were off scrounging the street for peppermint, butterscotch, and bubble gum pieces along with every other kid on Main Street.

The second fire truck was the big pumper rig which sprayed a mist heavy enough to cool off the crowd in the afternoon July sun, but light enough that you didn't need to head home to change clothes. Except for any kid who was still scouring the street for candy. The generally accepted rule was if you were in the street, you were fair game. And we're all very proud of the excellent aim of our firefighters.

Finishing up the parade came a long line of four-wheel-drive vehicles. How this particular tradition got started no one knows, but anyone who drives a Jeep or any other off-road four-wheeler is eligible to fall in line at the close of the parade. The City Council has not written anything down about this yet, but the unofficial rule is the driver has to wear a ball cap and sunglasses. You'll fit in better if you have a cooler strapped to the back of your rig with a few bungee cords. Big balloon tires are impressive and most importantly, don't wash your vehicle. The dirtier the better.

As the off-roaders roll down the street the crowd begins to thin. A few folks hang around and visit the shops or grab a meal. Some people head home and fire up their barbecues for family gatherings while others rest up before heading over to the fairgrounds for the fireworks display later in the evening.

But not Maxine and Clarence. Maxine sits on the bench beneath the shade of the Bell Tower and gripes to her husband about the parade. Too many kids this year, not enough horses. Alcohol should be banned, the trucks were too loud. The band was better last year, who was that in the convertible.

"Are we coming back next year?" asked Clarence.

"Of course! We can't miss this!" answered Maxine. "This is the best parade in the world!"

And Maxine was right.

The City Council announces that this year's Fourth of July Fireworks Show at the fairgrounds will begin at approximately 9:30 p.m. and would everyone stop talking about the time and just enjoy the show.

The theme is "America the Beautiful" and, as always, the display promises to be one rocket better than last year. Please remember to pick up your trash.

CHAPTER TWO

City Council Fireworks

City Council meetings are usually good for comical entertainment, but last month's discussion on the upcoming Fourth of July fireworks display at the fairgrounds was particularly enjoyable.

Mayor Carl Romano, who really was the mayor this year, but only because it was his turn, started the discussion with a straightforward complaint that the traditional 9:30 p.m. "blast off" was just too late to start a fireworks show. Though Carl was the owner and operator of The Hof Brau, An Armenian Deli, which was a business name that asked more questions than it answered, he did take his job as mayor seriously. And he was good at it too.

"The noise level at that hour would disturb older folks at home," Carl stated thinking of his constituents, "and youngsters just should not be up that late."

Council member Charles "Charlie" Tuttle, who had already had three turns as Mayor, was a self-described retired business owner. What Charlie was retired from was hard to determine. At one time or another Charlie and his wife, Charlotte, owned about half of the shops on Main Street: the hardware store, shoe shop, army surplus center, pharmacy, a few different places to eat, and at least two clothing stores. Those are just the places most folks know about, but there could be more. And though Charlie had sold off most of his interests after Charlotte passed, no one was sure which places were still his. And even though

Charlie may have sold the business, there was a high probability that he still owned the building.

Not that any of that mattered anyway, as Charlie was more visible and active in downtown activities than anyone else in town and he never missed an opportunity to protect his citizens.

So Charlie joined in the discussion suggesting that city staff craft a letter to be sent to the fairgrounds director politely requesting the fireworks celebration begin earlier, say 7:30 p.m. and conclude by 9:00 p.m., in respect of surrounding neighbors and allowing families to return home at a respectable hour.

Council member Carl "the other Carl" Snyder, who had been mayor twice before breaking up and alternating the reigns of Charlie, immediately spoke up insisting that a mere letter was not a strong enough statement. Carl is, was, and always has been an insurance salesman, which means he is pushy and likes to get everything in writing.

Carl felt the council needed to write a "Memorandum of Understanding" insisting, no demanding, that the fireworks event begin at 7:15 p.m. and everyone be cleared out of the fairgrounds by 9:00 p.m., which would really mean concluding the show by 8:00 p.m. to give everyone attending, both pedestrians and drivers, plenty of time to navigate their way out of the fairgrounds before closing up the place.

Nobody likes to be left out during these discussions, particularly Council member Dr. Marcus Gilbert. Marcus, much to his disappointment, had yet to take a turn as mayor and it is highly doubtful to anyone in the know that he ever will. Council members are elected by the public, but the mayor's position is selected each year by the members themselves. Dr. Gilbert was indeed a doctor, a Doctor of Chiropractic. Dr. Marcus Gilbert was a Doctor of Chiropractic from a time when every ridiculous, bizarre, or just plain strange story heard about Chiropractors was true. Dr. Marcus Gilbert did his best to live up to that reputation. And though he somehow managed to get reelected twice to the council, there was not much hope of him advancing to the big chair.

Marcus saw this moment as an opportunity to pass a resolution and create a new City Ordinance stating that "Public Fireworks Demonstrations, Events, and Displays shall begin at 7:00 p.m. and conclude no later than 8:00 p.m."

The four members kept the debate going for quite awhile. Lobbying for the most appropriate starting time, arguing about how long it really took to empty out the fairgrounds, and clamoring about which was the best method to put this plan in action.

The remaining council member, Deborah Singerman, was accustomed to these long winded arguments, so no one was surprised to see Deborah remain quiet during this session. Mrs. Singerman was a well-respected school teacher of twenty-five years. She had been elected to the council five times and served as mayor during year one of her second term. Wearing the hat of mayor did not appeal to her so she has passed up the offer several times. Deborah does feel she has something to offer both the council and the city so she keeps running for reelection. Apparently people agree, as she receives more votes than anyone else on the council.

Deborah's facial expression was not of boredom, impatience, or exasperation as might be expected. She looked calm, patient, and almost peaceful as she waited for a pause in the council's deliberations. Using that practiced demeanor that only a seasoned classroom teacher can have perfected, Deborah then spoke a single sentence as a voice of reason in the wilderness of bureaucracy.

Discussion on the Fourth of July fireworks demonstration was immediately stopped and the council moved on to other matters.

A little over three weeks later, on Sunday evening July 4th, the sun set about 8:45 p.m. and *the skies were dark about forty-five minutes later.* The fireworks were wonderful.

CHAPTER THREE

Mary and Carrot

Mary Thorpe never did care much for cats. Though she'd had quite a few over her eighty-plus years, they were mostly for the benefit of her two boys back when they were just a couple of youngsters. It wasn't that she was allergic to cats, she just didn't have any use for animals that left fur everywhere and didn't come when you called them. Not that she was fond of dogs either, or really just about anything in the animal kingdom. A good fifty years had passed since Mary had a cat in her home, so it came as a surprise when Mary agreed to look after her neighbor's cat, Carrot.

Carrot's owner, Trudy, a tall, big-boned Dutch woman with poor circulation, spent most days lying in bed keeping her ninety-two-year-old feet elevated above her head. Carrot, a not surprisingly orange, long-haired cat was the perfect companion. An independent, yet heat-loving feline who particularly enjoyed curling up around sock-covered ankles and toes. The two had shared twelve years together in their half of a modest one-story duplex. But as seasons change, the time came when Trudy and Carrot just could not handle living on their own. The twice weekly visits by the assistance folks and even the warm meals delivered several times a week were not enough. Distant family decided it was time for Trudy to move to an "Assisted Living Center."

Five years earlier Trudy might have put up a fight, but today she knew it was time. There would be no argument. There was, however, one true concern.

"What about Carrot?"

Mary Thorpe was born and bred in New England, a *very* nice part of New England. Some folks say that explains why she seems to walk around with her nose in the air and nothing is ever quite fine enough for her. But if they get to know Mary, they learn her mannerisms just mean she was raised in a proper fashion and she is accustomed to nice surroundings. As it happens, Mary was also a child of the Great Depression which meant she knew hard times, the value of two bits, and not to complain about what you no longer had. Which also helped explain why Mary never uttered a complaint about the last fifteen years in her half of the modest one-story duplex: a simple place with two bedrooms, one bathroom, a living room, a small kitchen with a separate dining room, along with a nice covered concrete patio, which Mary never used, in a pleasant backyard where she never went. A fine home, but a far cry from earlier times.

Visitors to Mary's home are stunned by the gorgeous collection of Eastlake antiques throughout the house. Among the highlights: walnut parlor chairs with inlaid detail, a drop leaf dining table with hand carving, dressers with original brass hardware, dovetail joints, and pink marble tops, and a pair of matching hand carved walnut sofas covered in pale blue velvet. And underneath or on the back of each furnishing was secured a paper stating the full name of which relative would receive this piece and the date the decision was made. Mary had watched plenty of friends pass and did not want to see her family squabble over who got what when her time came. Yet to Mary, this was just her furniture. The furniture and the home were a place for family and a few friends to sit, visit, and occasionally stay overnight.

Anyone looking inside one of the those drawers would find more evidence of someone who had survived the Depression.

Grabbing a napkin from a drawer might mean holding a refolded white paper napkin from the local Denny's in your hand with just a bit of lipstick or food smudge on the corner. Pulling out a placemat might find you looking at the selection of pies available at Marie Callenders twenty-five years ago, again with just a touch of a meringue stain implied from one of their delicious lemon pies. Mary saved everything.

Salt and pepper packets, tea bags- "you can use them more than once," plastic silverware, jelly and jam containers, and piles of ketchup packages. Mary saved everything. "You never know when you'll need one," she would explain. More than one person has listened to her advice on how to smear grape jelly on your husband's leg so the hole in his sock is not visible to anyone at his workplace. Mary's late husband, Elmer, passed on twenty years ago so there is no way to verify how often they used this technique, but after opening a few more cupboards and drawers around the house there does not seem any reason to doubt her story.

Mary's penchant for saving also applied to the dishwasher in her kitchen. "Why run that machine when you can just wash them by hand?" A fine sentiment toward saving both water and electricity, but not too hygienic when talking about the eyesight of a kind, but very old woman. Anyone who eats a meal at Mary's place has learned to check all dishes, silverware, and crystal for similarities to her napkins and then rewash as needed.

Oddly enough, Mary's poor eyesight was the key to both the success and frustration in her relationship with Carrot. Carrot, as with most cats, pretty much minds his own business. When Mary listens to talk radio, Carrot finds a window sill to stretch out in. If the television is on in the living room, Carrot finds a nearby spot on the carpet. Of course there is one exception, when Mary tries to read a paper or large print book, or decides to open a box of stationery and pen a letter to a friend, then Carrot wants to march through and across the papers meowing and scrunching as much as possible. But that is in the genetic structure of all cats and Mary is not able to do much reading or writing anyway.

The shedding fur of a long-haired orange cat on a pale blue antique sofa was a problem that did not exist because Mary is not bothered by what Mary can no longer see. Even the occasional Carrot pee or pile on the carpet was not a concern, as Mary's sense of smell was fading at a pace similar to her eyesight. Pees and piles, though, were a major concern for visiting grandchildren who had to add 'cleaning carpets' to the list of chores to be done on weekly visits.

The two roommates actually got on quite well. Mary picked up the habit of talking to Carrot. Not as a conversation, but as more of announcements or proclamations: "I'll go get the mail," "I'm having soup for dinner," or "I'm going to bed now."

But Mary was completely perplexed by one curiosity about this cat. Carrot was a front door cat. He would only enter and exit the house through the front door near the kitchen. Carrot would not meow or yowl when he wanted out, he would just calmly wait by the front door until Mary came to let him outside. This 'front door only' behavior was particularly bothersome because although Mary did not use her back porch or backyard, she kept the sliding glass door open quite often. She enjoyed the occasional cool breeze, which she said reminded her of her childhood. And to Mary's credit, her mind was sharp enough to know that old folks need to air out their home on a daily basis, even if they think they don't need to.

So to watch this silly cat just sit in the doorway of the open sliding glass door day after day and not go outside was bothersome. Carrot would just sit and stare, sometimes watching birds come right in the backyard and even hop on the back patio, yet he would never take a step outside. Mary found this habit so mystifying she became more annoyed with each day.

Finally, Mary had enough and decided Carrot would become a back door cat. Carrot just needed a little push to go outside and get some exercise and fresh air.

She nudged him with her foot, gently.

Nothing.

So, Mary nudged him again.

Carrot turned his head, but did not budge.

Mary prodded him a bit harder.

Again, Carrot twisted his head, but still no progress.

A third push got a twisted head, an irritated "meoooowrrrrr," and some nasty hissing, but no forward motion.

Mary did not get to near centurion status with a weak will and she certainly was not going to let a cat get the best of her, so while uttering her first offensive word in the last half century, "Go outside you damn cat!" she gave Carrot a final scoop shove with her shoe lifting the cat up and forward...

It was only then, when her shoe hit the closed screen door, that Mary realized why Carrot wouldn't go outside.

And the best part is listening to Mary giggle at herself when she tells the story.

The annual Pajama Day at the public library had to be canceled during the event last Saturday. Crying children and upset parents were seen leaving the building after Head Librarian Lacey Peabody asked everyone to leave and closed the facility around noon.

When asked Mrs. Peabody explained, "Pajama Day was intended to be for the children. Unfortunately some of our adult citizens are dressing rather immodestly."

Mother of two Gail Harrison was more direct scowling, "It was like a nightclub in there. Those people weren't there to check out a book."

"It was kinda like a Victoria's Secret catalog," admitted one smiling father who didn't want to be identified. "Maybe we can have a separate Pajama Night just for adults."

CHAPTER FOUR

The First Walt Story

Walter Peterson is a great man. Not cattle baron wealthy or Nobel Prize famous, at least outside of the neighborhood, but he is indeed a great man. Married for forty years to Barbara, which some would say that ability alone proves his stature; father of one daughter, Megan, who was lucky to survive the fifth, ninth, and seventeenth Walt stories, and; stepfather to two sons, Sandy and Kelly, (who never seemed to be in real physical danger themselves from any Walt stories, but one of them was generally close enough to be a good witness), who might as well be his boys by birth.

Walt is a retired Civil Engineer who spent his early career building concrete bridges and four-lane freeways for the State Division of Highways in Southern California. He then went on to building multilevel department stores for private developers and sewage treatment plants for the state before leaving California to build high-rise hotel and casinos during the end of the now classic Mob era in Las Vegas, Nevada right before the big corporations moved in. The next ten years were spent back in California building everything from office parks to college libraries.

A solid forty years of construction projects with no serious injuries, accidents, or even close calls. Forty years of clients paying Walt for his wisdom, experience, and expertise in designing, organizing, and constructing multimillion-dollar projects.

But Walt had a secret.

A secret he managed to keep from the construction world and those million-dollar clients for forty long years. A secret that only family and close friends were aware of.

Walt is a klutz. True, Walt is a lovable and entertaining klutz, but a klutz nonetheless.

Walt is the guy who lies down on his belly in the middle of a parking lot in Yosemite National Park with his 35mm Minolta camera focusing his telephoto lens to achieve the perfect photograph of a Steller's jay on a sugar pine branch. With vehicles honking and tourists staring, Walt will remain prone on the asphalt patiently waiting for the bird to turn his body and allow the light to best illuminate the features of his head. As cars maneuver around him and hikers step over him, Walt simultaneously depresses the button, captures a photo, and utters the familiar, "Gosh, Damn!" Two weeks later the ritual trip to pick up the photo at the pharmacy reveals a beautiful image of a bare sugar pine branch with yet another story of the one that got away.

Perhaps this klutziness has been an affliction since birth, but the condition has sustained itself for many years. To get to know Walt you really need to start with his first car.

Originally the car was a deep, lipstick red. But when Walt bought the vehicle five years used in 1965, it was already a rosy shade of pink. By the time early 70's arrived, you could tell the car had once been red, but now the little Volkswagen Karmann Ghia looked more like ink blots of crusty orange with hues of Pepto Bismol.

Walt had a key, but that would only open the door. Once inside, a large, flathead screwdriver was necessary to fill the ignition hole and start the engine. Any good size stick would have done the job as well, but the carburetor, fan belt, and emergency brake all seemed to prefer the amber handled, ten-inch Stanley that rested at the driver's feet. A simple, paint-splattered tool that knew every inch of the Ghia and fit Walt's palm better than any baseball glove ever could.

Black vinyl was attempting to pass itself off as a bucket seat on the passenger's side, but spongy, yellowed foam was escaping on all sides and total seam failure was eminent. On the driver's side the battle was over with the vinyl retreating to a new role of roving placemat that moved based upon the motions of the driver's rear end.

Riding with Walt in the Ghia was like sitting astride an aging power lawn mower where both driver and passenger are continually leaning forward to help both with momentum and to avoid dragging your bottom across the ground. Passengers could look through the floorboards and watch the highway pass beneath them in several places, with the best views by the stick shift, beneath the clutch, and where the driver's heel rests at the base of the gas pedal. Conversations were loud, frequent, and generally focused on: whether or not you would actually arrive at your destination; the safest way to get the car to the side of the road; whose turn it was to push, and; who to call for a ride that had not already been called that month.

Despite the flaws, the Karmann Ghia was a symbol. Perhaps a symbol of youth, or bachelorhood. Or maybe just symbolic of a lovable klutz.

The Ghia's am radio was scratchy but tunable, yet lately the baseball broadcasts had been replaced with the melodic sounds of the Carpenters. And when a certain lady was in the car, the soothing sounds of Roberta Flack, Barbra Streisand, and Neil Diamond were sure to be heard from the dashboard speaker. A change in radio stations, a change in relationship status, a change in job... could only lead to one event. A change in car.

Becoming engaged to Barbara, Barb: a widow, a widowed mother, a widowed mother with two boys; meant change. This new chapter of life demanded a new car, a reliable car. So the decision was made. Walt would sell his prized Ghia to long time buddy and about-to-be best man, Alan Brown. After much haggling and cajoling on the price, the two agreed that *Walt would pay Alan* one dollar to take ownership of the vehicle.

Transfer of title, which included the screwdriver, was to take place the day before the wedding, but Walt wanted one final trip with his Ghia. A short two-hour journey down the coast to celebrate the conclusion of bachelorhood with a few friends. The drive itself was uneventful with Walt arriving at Alan's girlfriend's house in San Diego well before five o'clock thereby avoiding the additional stress rush hour traffic can place on the Ghia.

Details of the party can be told another day. However, the basics involve a swimming pool, food, music, and alcohol, but absolutely no blindfolds, farm animals, or women paid under the table. Alan, his girlfriend Donna, along with a couple of dozen old friends and coworkers, joined in a traditional rite of passage for young American men. No arrests or convictions were made and there would be no story in the morning paper. The value of Heineken stock rose noticeably and a great time was had by all.

Sometime between The Stones and The Who or maybe it was during Dylan, Walt learned that he would not be able to spend the night at Donna's place. Barb was okay with the idea. Though she often had her doubts about Alan, she liked Donna and thought she was good for Alan. Barb was not the problem, but her mother, Louine, was appalled. A future son-in-law should not spend the night at a single woman's home. Despite Walt's present condition, he had the good sense to realize that ticking off the mother-in-law, who would be living a block away after the nuptials, was not the best way to begin a marriage.

Nearing midnight, Walt began drinking coffee, walking around, and swimming laps to wake up and clear his head. Coffee, walk, swim, and pee. Coffee, walk, swim, and pee. Walt kept the rehabilitation going several hours until he was feeling somewhat normal again. Now feeling wired and ready for the road home, Walt had Alan, who was oddly familiar with DUI tests, run him through a few checks. Alan pronounced him good to go. Once again showing his good sense in recognizing that Alan might not be the best person to make this judgement, Walt asked Donna, who had not been drinking, to check his condition. Once Walt had proven himself ready to roll, the partygoers sent their now highly caffeinated friend back on his way home.

Walt was wide awake and driving home with no problem. With the Ghia running smooth and no traffic he made good time heading north on the freeway for an hour and a half. Reaching town Walt pulled off the freeway and hit the surface streets for the last half hour home. About this time the physical exhaustion and caffeine let down conspired in an assault on Walt's senses. He was tired, with droopy eyes, sagging cheeks, and wobbly arms that no longer wanted to grasp the steering wheel. Though only thirty minutes from home, good sense reigned and Walt knew he needed to stop.

It was either the tapping on the driver's side window or the beam from the Policeman's flashlight, he wasn't sure which, that woke Walt from his much needed slumber.

Quite startled, he twitched and straightened out his legs, which until now had been quite relaxed with the left leaning against the door and the right comfortably tucked between the steering wheel and the stick shift. Scraping his left calf against the window crank with the cracked knob, Walt untangled himself and complied with the Officer's circling hand motion.

"What's the trouble Officer?" Walt asked in a groggy but respectful voice.

A somewhat puzzled public servant responded, "What are you doing sir?"

Walt explained that he had been out at a gathering earlier this evening and stayed quite late. He proudly added that even though it was only a short drive home, he realized that he was just too tired to drive. Therefore, the proper civic minded, responsible action to take was to stop driving and get some rest. Walt, now wide awake again and gushing with pride, looked to the patrolman for a thank you, a congratulatory statement, or perhaps some well-deserved high praise for his public safety thoughtfulness.

"Yes, you're right," agreed the Officer, "but the next time you want to stop driving and sleep, try pulling over to the side of the road."

CHAPTER FIVE

Sandy, Kelly, and the Pepper Tree

If your last name is Green and your first name is Kelly, you can be assured your parents had an interesting sense of humor. If your last name is Green, your first name Kelly, and you are male, then you also know your parents had a bit of a mean streak (or a really tough pregnancy).

Kelly Green never got a satisfying answer about the origin of his name from his mother Barbara, and since his father died back when Kelly was six years old there wasn't an answer to be found from him either. Barbara's response was simply that they liked unusual names, so he was "Kelly" and his brother was "Sandy." Besides, life is tough and boys need to develop hard heads and thick skin to make it through life. Comforting words from mother to son.

With these unisex names both boys endured years of teasing from schoolyard playmates. Certainly "Kelly Green" was a more colorful name and made Kelly an easier and more frequent target than his brother. Which Kelly tried to even out by often changing his brother's last name to "Beach." Kelly chanting "Sandy Beach, Sandy Beach!" on the playground or at one of Sandy's baseball games didn't make much sense to anyone else, but it infuriated Sandy which made Kelly feel a little better.

Two brothers bonded in the hatred of their names and in their love for a mother who wished for them to have hard heads and thick skin to survive life.

In the far right corner of Sandy and Kelly's backyard a Pepper tree grew. The evergreen, yet ever-dropping tree stood about thirty feet tall with a trunk just large enough for a young boy to hug and not quite touch his fingertips together on the other side. With a canopy thick enough and low enough to prevent anything from growing beneath except for a bit of moss on the hard-packed soil, this was the perfect spot to keep a pair of busy boys occupied.

Earth-moving Tonka trucks pushed aside leaves, berries, and small pebbles allowing for a metropolis to be born. Matchbox cars cut narrow tire track roads through the soil creating enough city streets and freeways to reenact every episode of The Rockford Files ever made. Any red vehicle capable of speed was apt to be a bad guy (Sandy), while the nondescript green Fords were always the FBI or undercover agents (Kelly). Many a crime was plotted, executed, and then solved in the world existing beneath that tree.

And watching it all, keeping the city safe, was a company of dark green, half-inch tall, plastic army men. Stationed on and behind protruding roots, the men were ready at a moment's notice to lend assistance as needed for crowd control, search and rescue operations, and major bank robberies involving hostage situations. High Command, run by Sandy, was also prepared to occupy the city as protection from the dreaded enemy company of light green, half-inch tall, plastic army men that were known to be stationed somewhere in the backyard.

Though they did not interact with soldiers or cars, the world beneath the Pepper tree was also filled with animals. The boys had numerous cats and dogs which survived without incident, but smaller creatures often had a rough life followed by a gruesome ending.

Guinea pigs, though messy, can be friendly, enjoyable pets. They squeak with personality, feel great to the touch, and eat just about any kitchen vegetable waste. Both male and female bite hard enough to hurt, but not deep enough to demand a trip to the emergency room for stitches. And after ten or thirty bites your skin toughens up which makes it more difficult for the rodent to penetrate your skin. As Sandy learned from the resulting litter of six pups, it is very challenging to tell the sexes apart, and yes, females can get pregnant again almost immediately. And apparently it is not unheard of for males to eat their young, so separating the boar from the babies might have been a good idea. The boys' mom, Barbara, was not about to have cannibals as pets. So much for the guinea pigs.

Rabbits, dwarf bunnies, were also great pets to keep in the land below the Pepper tree. Though a little shy in the personality department, rabbits are messy, feel great to the touch, and eat just about any kitchen vegetable waste. The ability to consume kitchen vegetable waste was always a key selling point in successfully arguing to obtain a pet in the first place. But as Kelly learned, rabbits need a hutch strong enough to withstand the unprovoked attack of the neighbor's, "I'm sorry. I don't know how he got loose," no good schnauzer. Even the added protection of both dark and light green, half-inch tall, plastic army men was not enough to protect Kelly's rabbits. So much for the rabbits.

The chipmunk episode was very short lived. Just know that the little guys were messy, felt great to the touch, and ate just about any kitchen vegetable waste. Unfortunately, the cute critters also had a tendency to be escape artists and their demise involved an incident with a power lawn mower which rendered both boys unable to mow the backyard for several months. So much for the chipmunks.

How a tortoise, which Kelly insisted on calling a turtle, escaped from a fully fenced area beneath the Pepper tree is a mystery. No holes in the fence and no tunnels under the fence were observed. As far as either boy knew there was no black market for turtles and they did not seem to be a pet coveted by the community. So where did the turtle go? The boys had absolutely no suspects, but would be on the lookout for someone who had recently acquired a pet which was not messy, felt great to the touch, and ate just about any kitchen vegetable waste. So much for the turtle...tortoise.

With so many deaths an animal memorial park beneath the Pepper tree should not come as a surprise. Among the many burial plots neatly lined up along the edge of the fence, were several cats, all of whom, shockingly, died incident free, natural deaths. Most notable, was Alfie, a fun loving, black and white, short hair who was given a special headstone on his passing. Alfie was Walt's cat, given to Walt as a kitten when Walt first joined the family as Barb's new husband and the boys' stepfather. As Alfie grew, Walt steadfastly refused to allow the cat to be "fixed." Even though Alfie was of another species, Walt just could not allow this procedure on a fellow male. Which was a fine decision at the time, until Alfie gave birth to a litter of four kittens. Thus, Alfie's headstone paid tribute to his unique ability to bear kittens and Walt's unique ability to sex cats.

The Pepper tree was also home to a wonderful tree house. Access to the tree house was easy enough, Sandy had simply nailed a few wooden planks right into the trunk of the tree. Sandy then built a bit of a lounge sticking out on one branch about eight feet off the ground and several feet away from the main trunk. Kelly crawled out on the lounge a few times and just sat there, but never really lied down. Sandy was the bigger, heavier brother and more comfortable taking risks with his body. So the lounge was really claimed as his territory to occupy.

Climbing up a few more branches brought you to a small platform. Large enough for two preteen boys to sit cross-legged and eat their peanut butter and sliced banana sandwiches, but not so large as to be noticeable from the ground. Being unnoticeable was a key feature for the brothers as this tree house was built without permits from both the city and, more critically, the mom.

Tired of knocking their heads against branches and needing more daylight on the platform, one day the boys brought some tools to the treehouse. A long-handled pruner and a pair of clippers would be perfect to clear out some headroom and open up a skylight in the top of the tree. Young boys and tools get along pretty well and it was not long before the two had carved out a significant hole in the canopy.

The view was amazing! Sandy and Kelly could both stand on the platform and survey the entire backyard. You could even see inside the kitchen through the window on the back of the house. Actually, the view was good of everyone's backyard. The Messenger's yard was the closest. Always so full of weeds that even a pair of grimy boys thought the place should be cleaned up. The Goldberg's dichondra lawn was only interesting because of how perfect it was. Never a leaf, weed, or human was visible on or near the lawn at any time. The Carlson's had a pool in their yard, complete with slide, diving board and Grecian-style planters filled with citrus trees surrounding the pool. Unfortunately, they also had tall spears of cypress trees around their fence line which the boys instantly realized would make any chance of catching twenty-one-year-old Cindy swimming or sunbathing when she was home from college just about impossible. But worth trying.

Standing on the platform, checking out the neighborhood, the thought occurred to Sandy that someone might be able to see the two of them sticking up out of the top of the tree. Kelly realized that their beloved Pepper tree now probably looked like a doughnut to anyone looking at them from above. Being observed from above by passing helicopters and small aircraft is a constant worry to all youth who have hideouts in their backyards. But the biggest concern, both boys recognized, would be mom. No doubt she would be pretty ticked off if she knew what her delightful boys had done to this poor tree.

So a plan was hatched to conceal the new treehouse skylight. The brothers swiped a scrap of plywood, four-feet by four-feet, from the garage and maneuvered the heavy board up the plank steps, around the major limbs, and on to the top platform. From there, they jammed the plywood into the surrounding branches and set all of the clippings and debris on top of the new ceiling in the treehouse.

The plan worked beautifully. Sunlight no longer broke through to the mossy ground below and the treehouse was safe from the prying eyes of neighbors, pilots, and random hot air balloonists. As the boys were celebrating their success they did not realize that in their placement of plywood above their heads they had neglected to consider certain environmental factors such as relative humidity, earthquakes, wind speed, gravity, and most importantly, curious cats.

Cats, as it turns out, are very adept at leaping off falling plywood and landing safely on nearby branches. Young boys' heads, as it turns out, are excellent targets for falling plywood squares loaded with the weight of freshly cut Pepper tree branches.

Barb, the boys' mother, who had been patiently observing every moment of this entire operation from a completely unobstructed viewpoint behind the kitchen window, waited for a crying pair of busy boys to come running in the back door. Though the boys did come inside with watery, red eyes and dirty, scratched faces, they swallowed their tears and never said a word to mom. For the first time it began to occur to Barb that Walt was having an impact on his stepsons, perhaps klutziness was not genetic, but environmental. Either way Barb saw she had a pair of hard-headed, thick-skinned boys who were developing just fine.

First grade teacher and City Council Member Deborah Singerman taught us all a lesson today about the need to be explicit with second language students. When Mrs. Singerman asked one of her students to write his name at the top of his paper he replied, "But I don't know how to spell my name."

Well, being prepared and planning ahead of time like all good teachers, Mrs. Singerman had labeled everything in the room and all belongings in the classroom with student names, so she wisely answered, "I put your name right there on the top of the crayon box. So you can copy that."

"Thanks!" replied the eager student.

Feeling good about her foresightedness, Mrs. Singerman smiled and didn't give the exchange a second thought until going through student work at the close of the day. That's when she discovered one student had written a rather unusual name at the top of every paper he had turned in...Crayola.

CHAPTER SIX

Kensington Gardens

As elderly ladies go, Mary Thorpe is a class act. A proud woman of New England stock and an independent woman too, since the passing of her husband Elmer some twenty years ago. Now in her eighty-second year, life was beginning to change.

Mary's eyesight, once sharp enough to watch over her two young sons play on the beach and clear enough to play a mean game of bridge, was now failing. She had difficulty reading packages to cook herself even simple meals. Reading mail and paying bills was an arduous task involving a bright table lamp and a large heavy magnifying glass. Laundry was a challenge since she could no longer see the dials on the washing machine and often could not see or even smell if her clothing was soiled anyway.

Mary lost both of her adult sons to heart disease a few years back, so grandchildren stepped up to the task of caring for her and maintaining her home. But the place was just too big to clean and care for. The extra time and expense involved in the upkeep of a home and landscaping is substantial, more so when considering the home offers features that Mary no longer uses.

Added to that was the undeniable fact that Mary was a little lonely. Now that she had figured out how to let her cat Carrot outside by opening the sliding screen door in addition to opening the sliding glass door, he was spending more time with the neighbors and their two young school age daughters, and less time curling up around Mary's feet.

All these factors led to the inescapable conclusion the time had come for Mary to give up her home and move into some type of care facility. This decision was not easy, but was fully agreed upon by everyone involved: grandchildren, friends, neighbors, and even Mary's doctors. Everyone agreed this was the correct decision. Everyone but Mary.

All five grandchildren knew finding the right place would be difficult, if not impossible. Grandma Mary loved her independence and would not give up her freedom without a fight. Thus, a plan was put into place to ever so slowly convince Mary that moving was the right course of action.

Step one turned out to be surprisingly easy. Getting rid of Mary's car, an old blue Mercury Comet in pristine condition. Mary had not driven the car herself in several years and liked the idea of passing on the old friend to someone who would take her out for a spin on a regular basis. She did not even walk out to the garage to say goodbye, which was quite a relief to grandson Tommy who had somehow managed to significantly scratch up the top of the Comet by repeatedly dropping the wooden garage door on the roof of the car the last time he borrowed the vehicle. Not that there was much to worry about anyway, as Mary was not tall enough to see the roof of her car. Even if she had been tall enough the current state of her vision would not have allowed her to see the damage. There did not seem to be any point in telling Mary, and the grandkids were just relieved step one worked so smoothly.

Step two involved a little manipulation of an old lady, but the deception was rationalized since everyone's heart was in the right place. Grandma Mary was taken on a tour of a local, and rather rundown, nursing home. Two residents to a dingy room, beds on squeaky wheels, scant furnishings, a shared bathroom, a long walk down a linoleum tiled hallway to the craft room, and another long walk down a linoleum tiled hallway in the other direction to reach the cafeteria. Residents wore gowns or night clothing as they sat in wheelchairs or scuffed their rubber tipped walkers while shuffling down the hallways. Standard issue employee uniforms included both hospital white clothing and disgruntled worker scowls. Mary knew her Eastlake antiques, pineapple post mahogany bed, and beloved blue love seat would not make the trip to this institution. Her treasured collection of hats, each neatly nestled within an artistic, individual box, would also be left behind.

The cold, unfriendly, antiseptic atmosphere was not the place where Mary wished to spend her remaining years. But just as she did in her earlier bridge games, Mary held her cards close, showing no anger or emotion during her tour. With her lower jaw clenched and her cloudy eyes fixed on the exit, she never noticed the tears rolling down the cheeks of her double granddaughter escort.

Originally step three was to consist of another tour of a similar, yet harsher establishment, but after an emotional grandchild huddle recounting the "success" of the uncomfortable day, step three was scrapped. On to step four: Kensington Gardens.

Approaching Kensington Gardens for the first time makes a visitor of any age wish they were able to live in such a beautiful environment. The circular driveway takes you past lush green lawns, vibrant flower beds, and gently spraying water fountains inviting you to park your vehicle beneath the two-story porte-cache. While no valet is waiting to take your keys or carry your bags, the tone of elegance is assured before stepping inside the main entrance.

Grand ceilings with sparkling chandeliers, enormous parlor areas with comfortable sofas, and intimate corners with high back wing chairs combine to create a formal, yet warm, welcoming atmosphere. Though Mary did not play, her eyesight was still strong enough to capture the ambiance added to the room by the presence of a grand piano. One granddaughter thought she detected widened eyes and the other believed she felt a quickened pulse, but Mary said nothing.

A well-dressed young woman named Amber approached and introduced herself to Mrs. Thorpe. Oddly enough Amber addressed the two granddaughters by name without introduction. If Mary noticed, she did not say. Amber offered to take the ladies on a tour beginning with a typical home that Mary might select. The use of the word *home* appealed to Mary as she took Amber's arm.

Walking down the carpeted hallway Amber paused to show Mary the den. A nicely wood-paneled room with leather furnishings, excellent lighting, and a wall full of books. Amber explained anyone was welcome to read, relax, or study in the den anytime.

Across the hall was a similar styled room which Amber noted was the listening room. Here were record albums and compact discs featuring music for any taste from Sinatra's "I've Got You Under My Skin" to Springsteen's "I'm On Fire" and Beethoven's "Moonlight Sonata" to The Beatles "Magical Mystery Tour." Amber mentioned that sometimes grandchildren and great-grandchildren visited this room and once the door was shut the room was completely soundproof.

Continuing down the brightly lit hall past several eye-catching crystal wall sconces brought the ladies to home number 124. A turn of the key and a step inside revealed a lovely home. The living room was just a tad smaller than Mary's current home. Mary saw that there would not be room for all of her furnishings, but a cherished love seat, coffee table, and pair of wingback chairs would easily fit. When Mary commented the dining area and kitchen were rather small, Amber quickly explained the kitchenette and eating area was really just for the homeowner's convenience for a cup of tea or late-night snack. Most people ate their full meals in the Kensington Gardens Dining Room.

Amber mentioned a two-bedroom home was available, but the single-bedroom model they were looking at now had a more spacious master bedroom. One bedroom, large enough to hold a pineapple post bed, along with a walk in closet featuring one wall of floor to ceiling shelves. Shelves which Amber just happened to mention were deep enough to hold shoeboxes or those lovely hatboxes that some women collect. This single-bedroom model also included a small outdoor patio accessed by a sliding glass door with a sliding screen. Mary's giggle at the mention of the sliding screen was lost on Amber, but made her granddaughters smile.

The giggling grandma was the first definitive sign that Mary might indeed be interested, but the best selling point was yet to come. Amber suggested they walk to the Kensington Gardens Dining Room. As they walked back down the hallway Amber showed Mrs. Thorpe a few additional features of the facility. A craft room which was often used by quilters, but was also used for teaching classes for those looking for new hobbies. They also passed a beauty parlor which Amber explained worked on an appointment system. Of course, if you had your own stylist in town the Kensington Gardens minibus would take you to your hair appointment or any other appointment you might have. The air conditioned minibus also took several trips a week for downtown shopping excursions as well as trips to the mall at the edge of town.

Walking in the Kensington Gardens Dining Room Mary discovered this was no cafeteria. This room was designed as a full service restaurant. Comfortable booth seating as stylish as any nice place in town lined the exterior of the room, while drop leafed tables for four to six diners filled the interior space. There was no self-service buffet line here. Well-groomed youth worked as wait staff, seating you at a table, presenting you with menus in addition to sharing the specials of the day. And the residents dressed up for meals! Amber shared early arrivals tend to be more casual, but those seated later would find gentlemen in coats and ladies, wait for it, wearing hats!

Mary politely expressed her appreciation to Amber for the tour. Amber thanked Mrs. Thorpe for visiting and assured her she would be happy to answer any questions she might have. Mary acknowledged with a nod, then began quickly walking toward the front entrance with her granddaughter escorts a step behind. Both granddaughters exchanged a bewildered look between them speculating on the motive for Mary's hastened pace. Once outside under the porte-cache granddaughter Jennifer asked, "Where are you going in such a hurry?"

Mary replied, "You're taking me shopping. I'm going to need a new hat."

CHAPTER SEVEN

Maxine and Clarence

Maxine and Clarence Baxter are great neighbors. They will do just about anything to help. If you need a tool of any sort, Clarence is your man. He will not only loan you the correct size screwdriver you need, but he will sharpen the blade of the wrong size screwdriver you did have along with the blades on your pruning shears and lawn mower while you wait. Clarence, at ninety-four, doesn't talk much and he doesn't move fast, but he is an efficient and knowledgeable source of information on repairing any item around the house. In that little workshop of his can be found nearly every woodworking and lawn tool that has ever appeared in the Sears catalog.

Though he is a bit old to help with the heavy physical work, Clarence is a tremendous resource to consult with *before* starting a project. So long as you *remember* to consult with him before starting a project. If by chance you start or finish a project without seeking his services, Clarence is sure to gingerly rise from his chair on the front porch, calmly set his cigar aside, and mosey on over to check out your progress. Whereupon he will state: "You know, you could have used my power spray gun and painted that picket fence in less than a tenth the time it took you to do it by hand," or "My belt sander would have planed that door right down to size," or perhaps "I got a rototiller that would have charged right through that hard packed soil instead of you shoveling all day like that." The timing of Clarence's comments are sometimes hard to take, but they are always right on the money.

While Clarence is really the expert on anything tool or repair related, Maxine is the expert, and authority, on everything else. And if you don't believe her, just ask and she will set you straight. Though nine years younger than Clarence (she loves talking about the scandal of getting married at fifteen), Maxine has more advice, experience, and opinions than her husband of seventy years or any sizable group of husbands could ever hope to have. Maxine is no busybody and she'll respect your privacy, but make no mistake, she will tell you what is on her mind and what you should do about it.

When young newlyweds Rob and Jennifer Taylor moved in to the 1907 Craftsman bungalow next door, they were impressed with the beautiful flower and vegetable garden Maxine and Clarence tended in the plot between the two houses. Fortunately for Rob and Jen, the first thing they did was ask for advice on setting up a garden.

Maxine started with a "how to" lesson. How to build a portable green house to get your seedlings started early, protect them from frost, and avoid wasting money on nursery plants you could grow yourself. All you needed were some scrap pieces of lumber, a bit of plastic sheeting, and a staple gun. Just a bit of work, a few packets of seeds, and a little sunshine, and there were happy seedlings at a fraction of the cost. Maxine was right.

The next lesson was on which variety of tomatoes to grow: Better Boys for sandwiches, Romas for salads, Golden Pears for munching while working in the garden, and a few heirloom varieties for unique juicy flavor. Just a bit of work, a little weeding, some water, along with lots of sunshine, and there were enough tomatoes to make salsa for the north side of town. Maxine was right.

More lessons followed on canning peaches, making blackberry jam, growing peppers, choosing the right fig, dusting grapes, cooking a compost pile, chasing neighborhood cats out of the garden, and how to grow dahlia and peony blossoms the size of dinner plates. And with every lesson learned you came to an inescapable truth. Maxine was right.

When neighbors try to return the favor and help out Maxine and Clarence with some work on their place, it can't be done. They are just too proud to accept help from neighbors. One evening when Rob could no longer stand the Tuesday night ritual of watching Maxine lug her two loaded trash cans to the top of the driveway, he snuck over and took them out to the street himself. He had nearly finished when Maxine came out yelling and barking and only halfway kiddingly bashing him in the back with a long handled push broom. No doubt Clarence had gained volumes of wisdom during his long tenure on earth with Maxine and one lesson he learned early on, that Rob was learning too, was to stand aside and stay out of Maxine's way.

Maxine is a proud and protective woman. She likes to talk about the old days and how she raised four kids, all boys, in this pint-sized 1,000 square foot, two-bedroom, one-bathroom cottage she and Clarence had been living in for almost seventy years. And she always brags that she did the child rearing without a shotgun. The Baxter boys knew how to behave. That is still true today as the "boys," all grandparents themselves, still make frequent phone calls and visits on a regular basis. In fact, those visits are the best opportunity for anyone to help out Maxine and Clarence.

The first full moon after the last chance of frost, usually mid-April to mid-May, finds the whole Baxter family pitching in to get the year's garden in the ground. Why the full moon you ask? You might conjecture on the relationship between the earth and the moon in regards to gravitational pull, but Maxine will tell you, "Because that's when you put in the garden." And don't argue because by now you know Maxine is right.

Sons pushing the tiller and hoeing rows, grandsons and granddaughters driving stakes and digging holes, great-grandchildren planting seedlings and setting tomato cages, all make the garden a busy place. With Clarence on the porch smoking his evening cigar and Maxine in the center of everything supervising workers, directing traffic, and teaching young ones how to run string to make a support fence for green beans, the activity is kept organized. Yes, those Baxter boys know how to behave. Children, grandchildren, and great-grandchildren are family members and therefore exempted from the rules about helping that apply to Rob, Jen, and other well-meaning neighbors.

Maxine and Clarence do have one neighbor who tests their patience. Kevin O'Malley, a wheelchair-bound veteran, lives in a small shack of a house, much less than half the size of the Baxter place, right next door. Right next door means right next door. The space between Maxine's bedroom and Kevin's place is just wide enough to squeeze in Clarence's old Dodge pickup, so long as any passenger doesn't mind sliding over on the bench seat and climbing out through the driver's side door.

Kevin tends to be on the quiet and grumpy side. He'll nod a hello at you as he rolls by, but never a smile or a wave of the hand. The lack of a wave could simply be because his gloved hands are always busy on those wheels, but the absence of a friendly smile was more of a mystery. You might think his sullenness in face was due to his inability to move his legs, but you'd be wrong. Kevin had long since accepted his paralysis as a soldier's badge of honor and the payment he'd made for saving the life of a friend. The bitterness on his face stems from his daily frustration with rolling his chair down such a bumpy street and if he stops to chat, it is that much harder to get his momentum going down the street with all the unfilled cracks and potholes. Other than that explanation, Kevin is a quiet and grumpy person because Kevin is a quiet and grumpy person.

Of course the only neighbor who knew those reasons behind Kevin's grumpiness was Maxine. Being next door, she was in the position to have more conversations when Kevin was just outside and not headed anywhere in particular. Being married to a veteran herself Maxine had a bit of a soft spot for Kevin. Plus, she could be a pretty good grump herself and she recognized what they had in common. The rest of the neighborhood just saw a grumpy guy who played extremely loud music that appeared to make the exterior walls of both his home and neighbors eardrums swell and contract with the alternating beat of the bass. Nearby children wanted the chance to pet his yellow lab, but had learned the loyal dog was too busy keeping his head down just below the seat of Kevin's chair following his master. And if the dog did start to wander over for a friendly head scratching he was sure to get a zap from his electric collar. The dog received the zap, not the child.

Like all the neighbors, Maxine did not like the loud music, the dog howling, or the noisy cars and guests that always showed up on Friday and Saturday nights. But what she disliked the most was Kevin's job. Kevin worked at home cleaning and repairing guns for a living: revolvers, rifles, shotguns, anything that could be fired.

Of course, fixing guns means testing guns, which means firing guns. Which means noise. Which helps to explain why Kevin often had his music turned up so loud. Which further explains that the headphones Kevin often wore while his music was blasting the neighborhood, were not stereo headphones, rather they were ear protection headphones for him to wear while he was blasting guns. That piece of information would have explained a lot to perplexed neighbors who were curious about a guy listening to music through headphones while anyone within a quarter mile could hear the music just fine without the headphones.

Kevin had a bullet recovery system, a fancy device known as a Cotton Box, as well as a sound deadening system, for use when firing a revolver, that did help some. But Maxine was never crazy about a guy firing guns ten feet away from her bedroom window. Kevin had received many strong lectures from Maxine about the timing of his shots interfering with phone calls, dinner, and the regular rate of her heartbeat. The sound of Maxine's scratchy, craggy, booming old voice eventually won out and the two finally reached a cease fire of sorts, coming to agree that Kevin would be more aware of his impact on others and he would definitely not fire any weapons when the grandchildren were around.

The treaty lasted a few months until Kevin accidentally discharged a high-powered rifle outside his fancy Cotton Box. The shot blasted through Kevin's exterior wall, Maxine and Clarence's exterior bedroom wall, and lodged in the opposite interior bedroom wall eighteen inches above the walnut desk that held a Singer sewing machine. Which meant the bullet had passed no more than two inches above the left shoulder of the lady sitting at the walnut desk working on the machine sewing a patch on her husband's denim overalls.

Who got outside first was difficult to determine. It might have been Maxine, storming and swearing with enough force to make a sailor blush, or it could have been Kevin, looking both pale and relieved at the same time. But thank goodness it was probably Clarence using all his might to break his long standing rules and hold back his firebrand wife. You could not understand everything Maxine was yelling, but the gist of her message was clear enough. Though his voice was shaky, Kevin's profuse apologies were coming quickly but did little good.

Maxine's voice blasted out stronger than any of Kevin's firearms, "This is *exactly* the reason I don't own a gun!"

Kevin kept trying to explain, "I'll fix everything!" mixed in with, "Are you hurt?" followed by, "This was an accident!"

Maxine barked back, "You don't get it Kevin. This is *exactly* why I don't own a gun. If I owned a gun, you'd be dead right now and it *wouldn't* be an accident."

And Maxine was right.

Local police briefly detained an unidentified male when he was found trespassing after hours in the auto junkyard section of the county dump yesterday. After explaining he had just come to say goodbye to an old friend and collect a screwdriver, authorities released him with no charges.

He was granted custody of the screwdriver.

CHAPTER EIGHT

The Second Walt Story

The second Walt story did not hurt anyone, except Walt of course, and actually ended on a positive note. You may know Walter "Walt" Peterson as an exemplary civil engineer, a great neighbor, or as an all around good guy. But you may not be aware that Walt is an accident prone klutz. He has managed to hide this fact from just about everyone but family and close friends.

You definitely noticed Walt's gray front tooth that stood front and center, fully visible every time he flashed his friendly and frequent smile. If you ever asked Walt about the tooth you would likely get a shrug and slightly embarrassed look followed by a brief nondetailed explanation of an accident he had as a sixteen-year-old high school student involving a trampoline. The tooth slowly grayed over time and Walt just gradually accepted the situation until he never thought about it at all. Some folks might have just thought this to be an innocent accident of youth, and not suspect that this was really one early incident in a lifetime of self-inflicted wounds by a lovable klutz. As for other folks, once they got to meet Walt, they never thought about the gray front tooth either. They just liked the man and his character.

That character was never more evident than in Walt's choice of a wife. After years of trolling the Belmont Shore and Huntington Beach Southern California social scene, Walter met Barbara. A woman five years his senior, during a time well before marrying a cougar was fashionable. And this cougar already had kits, two boys. Sandy, a twelve-year-old who had become accustomed to being the man of the house after the death of his father, who was not interested in having a stepfather. And Kelly, an eight-year-old who had become accustomed to borrowing everyone else's dad, who was interested in having a stepfather.

Despite the strong objections of Walt's aging mother, who had always hoped that her son Walter Francis Peterson would return home to his roots in Connecticut and marry a nice Catholic girl, the wedding did take place. Though mom did not attend, the East Coast Petersons were represented by a few of Walt's distant cousins.

Although a few side bets were made as to whether Walt's best man Alan would last to the end of the ceremony without passing out, the wedding itself was a success. The previous night's bachelor party left Alan three shades of green, but the groom himself was in good shape and never missed a cue.

A relaxing two-week honeymoon in Acapulco ended with selecting gifts for a pair of anxious boys who were waiting back home for a souvenir from Mexico. On the way to the airport Walt and Barb stopped at a roadside gift stand and picked out a stuffed armadillo for Sandy, which was promptly confiscated in the airport as being an endangered animal and was therefore illegal to take out of the country. The argument of "But it's already dead!" did nothing to alter the minds of Mexican officials. The knowledge that the confiscated armadillo was most likely now on his way back to the same roadside gift stand to be resold to the next unsuspecting tourist made Walt and Barb wonder just how well traveled was this little armored mammal. Turtles, however, were apparently abundant in Mexico and did not merit status as endangered animals as Kelly did receive his stuffed green water turtle.

Barb brought home the other souvenir from the honeymoon in Mexico... morning sickness. As well as afternoon and evening sickness. A case of stomach flu, food sickness, or Montezuma's Revenge for the ages. Intestinal discomfort that had not been reached in her lifetime and would not be attained again until one summer morning seventeen months later.

That was the morning Barb presented, though attacked might be more accurate, Walt with a small box the moment his eyelids first gave sign he might be awake. A groggy husband opened the gift to discover a pair of freshly knitted booties, one pink bootie and one blue, with a note stating the arrival of a new little Peterson in approximately seven months. There was also a promise to knit one more bootie of the appropriate color as the day came closer.

Being the organized lady she is, Barb not only had the second bootie ready, she also had multiple hats, sweaters, mittens, and blankets knitted for the child's first two years of life. Every item was hand knitted, every item was pink, and every item was ready when Megan Peterson joined the world on January 28th.

A mere two months later a family meeting was called. Southern California had now reached its carrying capacity for building multilevel department stores and Walt was given a choice by his bosses in the construction world. The family could either move to Phoenix, where Walt could continue the construction migration of multilevel department stores into Arizona, or the family could move to Truckee, where Walt could build a sewage treatment plant. Ignoring the potential humor or disgust in building a facility that treats raw sewage, the first question asked by all, except for Megan, was, "Where is Truckee?"

Once the choice was clear between living in the unbearably hot, parchingly dry desert in the middle of Arizona or the lush green, snow covered peaks of the Sierra Nevada Mountains a mere dozen miles north of Lake Tahoe, the decision was obvious. For the next two years Walt would be the civil engineer building a sewage treatment plant and Barb, Megan, Sandy, and Kelly would get to experience life in the mountains.

Leaving the family behind, Walt headed up to the Sierras a month early to pick out a place to live. Having grown up in Connecticut, Walt was experienced in dealing with snow, and mountain life in Truckee might have been fine if Walt had applied that experience in picking out a place to live. Unfortunately, Walter Peterson brought his "I've been living near the ocean in sunny, Southern California for the last twenty years," experience to the situation and selected a home that might have been perfect if the house was sitting on the coast with a gorgeous view of the never-ending Pacific Ocean. But it wasn't. This house was in the Sierra Nevadas, just shy of the seven thousand foot elevation mark.

Built on concrete pilings so the floor of the home was four feet off the ground, the front appearance looked quite impressive. Sandy and Kelly both remarked how they had never seen underneath a house before. And when you drove up to the home you could see clear through beneath the house to the manzanita and ponderosa pines on the other side. The house was a two-story, 1800 square foot home with cathedral ceilings and tilt-up wall construction. Tilt-up simply means the walls of the home are pre-assembled in another location, brought to this site, and tilted up into place with the help of a small crane.

Once inside, the house became even more impressive. The entire back wall was a collection of floor to ceiling windows with several sliding glass doors at the base topped by a series of four-foot by six-foot glass panels reaching all the way to the peak of the second story. As each glass panel reached the sloped roof, an additional triangular panel of glass filled the space to capture maximum sunlight and allow a truly unobstructed view from inside the house. The second floor of the home included an interior balcony which overlooked the living room below and the entire back wall of glass, *single pane* glass. Simply beautiful. A beautiful *summer* house.

When a family pet runs away or disappears everyone is upset. When two leave you become worried. But when all three family cats deserted the Peterson family after a few weeks in their new home, perhaps the event should have been taken as a warning or foreshadowing of perils to come. Yet when the first snowstorm of winter hit Truckee, all three cats returned without any explanation as to where they had been or what they had been doing. So the smiles in the house were plentiful heading into the first storm of the season. Even the smile with the gray front tooth.

Sierra storms tend to be windy. They gather moisture over the Pacific and then dump that moisture in the form of snow. Lots of it. But before that snow piles up, the wind really whips, gusting to 90 -100 miles per hour. And if your house is built up on concrete pilings with no skirt to connect your house to the ground and block that wind, there are consequences. Most notably, the water pipes freeze.

Thus one of the first winter jobs in the home became setting out the portable electric space heaters each night before going to bed. The first person up in the morning had the job of turning on the space heaters just behind the toilets and beneath the kitchen sink so the rest of the family could use the facilities and make breakfast, generally in that order. While some children crossed their fingers for deep snow around their house in hopes of getting a day off from school, Sandy and Kelly hoped for deep snow around their house so the snow would block the wind, the pipes would not freeze, and they would be free to flush the toilet first thing in the morning.

Even the casual observer might note, "Wait a minute. Wouldn't the wood stove keep the house warm during the night?" Mountain homes throughout the Sierras and other mountain ranges around the world have been kept warm throughout the night for years heating with wood. And since

Ben Franklin invented that great potbelly stove to keep the coals fresh overnight, a homeowner just opens the door to the stove and tosses in another log. All true. If the house has a wood stove.

This house, at near seven thousand feet in elevation, where all the local streets were named after cities in Switzerland, had no wood stove. Walt had selected a house with a standard open fireplace. Now it did have a homemade burn-a-lator. A burn-a-lator is a clever device where pipes are laid at the bottom of your fireplace, in theory sucking in the cold air along your floor. An electric fan pulls that cold air through the pipes beneath, behind, and finally above the fire burning in your fireplace. And voila! Warm air is blown throughout your home. Unless your home has two-story cathedral ceilings, which means being downstairs can require long sleeves, sweaters, and woolen socks, while the upstairs interior balcony demands more tropical attire.

Undoubtably the heating unit does a great job cutting the chill in the air at your beachfront estate along the Malibu coast. In the mountains, the unit makes your fire burning area much smaller and leaves you with no way to regulate air intake and control the speed with which your fire burns. Consequently, you have to add logs often and have absolutely no hope of making a fire or coals that will last even a third of the way through a cold winter's night. However, the machine does do an excellent job of blowing soot throughout your home. Unless of course the power goes out.

Thus, a second winter job was to get the morning fire started as soon as possible. Every family member, except Megan, became first rate and darn quick fire builders.

Four members being born in the warmth of Southern California meant this family was going to need a lot of wood to survive a Sierra winter. Family outings changed from trips to the beach with Coppertone lotion, flip flop sandals, and inflatable rafts, to trips to the woods with McCulloch chainsaws, red handled axes, and a flatbed truck. All wood cutting supplies and the vehicle were generously loaned from the construction site of the new sewage treatment facility courtesy of the new civil engineer.

The land in front of the Peterson house soon began to look like several families of beavers had taken up residence. Log piles of Douglas Fir, Ponderosa, and Tamarack were numerous and growing at a rate inverse to the rate of the boys belief that there was once a time they actually enjoyed playing with Lincoln Logs. Wood was expensive, so spare family time was spent felling marked trees, cutting logs to appropriate length, and then splitting each log to fireplace size.

Any family that burns wood for heat goes through lots of wood. The Peterson family burned through twenty cords of wood that first winter. Perhaps the cause was the two-story wall of single pane glass, the open fireplace with no method to control air flow, or the lack of knowledge that oak burns hotter and slower than pine. Or it might have been the fact that two of the tilt-up walls did not actually tilt up and touch each other at the top of the cathedral ceiling. Daylight peered in the inch-wide, ten-foot-long crack as easily as heat escaped. Whatever the reason, Walt was well aware of all the faults with this house and he was not about to let his family freeze.

A cord of wood is technically defined as a tightly stacked pile of split wood four-feet tall, four-feet wide, and eight-feet long or any other stacking configuration that equals 128 cubic feet. Generally speaking, a cord of wood is an overloaded eight-foot bed of an old, full-size Chevy pickup with raised fences or rails on the sides, and the truck should be riding a little low when it shows up in your driveway. If the wood only stacks to the top of the truck bed, you need two loads to make a cord. If you have one of those new pretty trucks with a six-foot bed, you need four loads to make one cord. Any way you stack it, twenty cords is a lot of wood.

Walt was naturally chief lumberman in charge of production. He did plenty of work with the chainsaw and handled all of the axe work. Sandy was old enough to respect the power of the chainsaw and use the tool with proper care and respect. Kelly was lead stacker and good at dragging just about anything from point A to point B. Barb was in a support role, charged with nursing Megan, keeping the three lumbermen properly hydrated, and maintaining the fire in the house.

After a long day of everyone fulfilling their duties, the full moon became the culprit behind Walt's decision to split a few more logs to top off the newest stack of firewood. The brightness of the moon reflecting off the surface of the snow made for the right conditions to squeeze in a bit more work before coming in for dinner. Kelly joined him setting one log at a time on the chopping stump, ready for Walt to swing the red handled, single bladed axe splitting each log in two. Kelly carefully placed each log, stood back, and then collected and stacked the split wood. The pair of lumbermen worked well together, each staying out of the other's way and steadily adding to their final product.

Until Walt brought the axe down through the night sky and into the next log. The axe blade hit a knot and the log refused to split. In fact the axe was now jammed into the knot and log so tightly Walt could not remove the axe. Even another overhead swing of the axe, with the log still attached, made no progress in removing the blade. Wiggle it out? No luck. More overhead swings? Wouldn't budge.

"What about the chainsaw?" suggested Kelly. A question that really ups the ante in disaster potential for this story, but you're apt to be comforted by Walt's response.

"Too late in the evening." replied Walt. Which was probably a good decision even though using a chainsaw might have prevented what happened next.

Normally when hitting a knot, you remove the axe and toss the offending piece of wood aside to deal with another day. If the woodcutter is motivated by the challenge or offended by the stubborn log, the second course of action often taken is to remove the axe and replace the position of the blade with a wide, metal wedge. A heavy, long handled sledge hammer is then used to drive the wedge through the knot. Problem solved.

Walter Peterson, of course, was both challenged and offended.

Unable to remove the axe, Walt decided to use the sledge directly on the back flat head side of the axe. Walt mightily swung the sledge overhead and came down on that axehead like John Henry driving a railroad spike. As metal hit metal, the blade of the axe drove through the knot exploding the log. Wood shrapnel flew everywhere with shards of pine going in all directions. Kelly was at the edge of the blast zone and was only hit with light debris. But Kelly was close enough to hear a string of words never heard before, and close enough to see the moonlit white snow was no longer white. The crisp, white snow was now a deeper red than any cherry snow cone Kelly had ever seen. Unlike John Henry, Walt was still standing but was covered with blood on his face, hands, and clothes. Cradling his mouth, spitting blood, and holding a tooth in his hand, the next words uttered were, "Don't tell your mother." As if she would not notice this bloody mess walking in the house.

Despite the volume of blood, Walt was only seriously hit by one piece of wood. A pine projectile that launched straight up from the knot and rocketed directly into his mouth. Call it karma, kismet, or the dumb luck of a lovable klutz, but that missile found only one target. Walt's gray front tooth.

Using clean, unbloodied snow, a stunned Kelly helped Walt wash up a bit before heading into the house. When Barb saw Walt, with absolutely no panic in her voice, she sprang into action. Remembering something she had read about the best chance to save a lost tooth was to put it right back in place, she took Walt into the bathroom, cleaned him up a bit more, and then attempted to slide the tooth back in place. Which was easier said than done. After a few painful and unsuccessful attempts Walt was ready to give up. But after looking at himself in the mirror and realizing he might have to move to Alabama and change his name to Bubba, Walt was willing to try again.

With the help of a few shots of Jack Daniels, the tooth did wiggle its way back into place. Leaving the boys behind to care for Megan, Barb and Walt rushed off to the emergency room where the Doc quickly double-checked the cleaning and pronounced they had done everything right. "Now we just have to wait and see if the tooth survives the trauma. Just leave it alone for awhile and don't use it for anything. Absolutely no apples!"

Within a month not only was the tooth firmly in place, right where it belonged, but the gray was fading! A healthier and better looking tooth was sitting front and center. The local dentist said it was rare, but not unheard of, for a traumatic shock to wake up a tooth and increase the blood flow to the surrounding nerves.

Just as none of Walt's friends really noticed the presence of his gray front tooth, now, none of his friends noticed the absence of his gray front tooth. That winter passed with a healthy and well-exercised family. Walter Peterson, the lovable klutz, felt proud keeping everyone happy and warm. You could tell by the smile on his face.

CHAPTER NINE

"Hey Grandma!"

Due to fading eyesight and other concerns, octogenarian Mary Thorpe recently moved from her beloved, spacious duplex of the last fifteen years into an assisted living facility. Anyone who has been through this experience with aging parents or incapacitated loved ones knows the pain and stress associated with this stage of life. Despite Mary's initial fears of giving up her freedom and independence, her transition was made less traumatic by her ability, with her grandchildren's help, to afford the stylish and posh Kensington Gardens.

Most residents were drawn in to Kensington Gardens by the pleasant koi ponds and lush landscaping and stayed because of the friendly staff and wonderful amenities. Mary knew she would be appreciative of the weekly laundry and maid services. She was also interested in both the on-site hair salon and the listening library. And riding the minibus downtown for shopping excursions with new friends would certainly be enjoyable. But the real selling points for Mary Thorpe were two items. First, the walk-in closet had floor to ceiling shelves which were the perfect depth for storing her treasured hat collection. And second, the Kensington Gardens Dining Room had a well-established tradition of diners dressing in semi-formal attire allowing Mary the perfect opportunity to wear her lovely hats.

Though Mary was excited when she signed the lease agreement with Kensington Gardens she did have one condition for her loving grandchildren. This move would be done on a trial basis for a few months, so she would not sell her duplex. She had already sold her car, and did agree to giving away some furnishings and household items that she no longer used. But she would not sell the duplex. All five grandchildren, who shared responsibility caring for Grandma Mary since the death of both their father and Mary's other son, were cautiously optimistic.

Parting with even portions of eighty-two years of possessions is another emotional trauma in this stage of life. Every item has a story and every story needs an audience.

Over two weeks each grandchild took a turn listening to those stories while helping Grandma Mary sort, share, give away, and pack. Sometimes laughing and sometimes smiling with an old woman who was a child of the depression. Giggling at her drawers full of unused ketchup and jelly packages rescued from years of visiting local Denny's and other coffee shops. Smiling at her memories of patching holes in the bottom of shoes with newspaper and smearing jelly on her husband's leg so no one could see the hole in his sock.

Sometimes crying with an old woman who had lost the three most important men in her life. Elmer, her husband of forty years whom she had built a life with. Two adult sons, James and Edward, whom Mary always assumed would outlive their mother. Grandmother and grandchild sorting through stories and photographs of four lifetimes.

Sometimes a grandchild just needed to listen and nod, concentrating on not nodding off, as Grandma Mary retold the same story of getting her first set of kitchenware. Proudly buying a new plate, platter, or drinking glass once a week at Krause's Market for two years until she had a full service for ten. A story all the grandchildren knew by heart and could retell in their sleep.

And sometimes a grandchild would be stunned listening to a piece of family history never heard before. As Grandma Mary explained she had another child. A third son, William, who died as a toddler in an accidental drowning. William was actually the first-born son and when he died she and Elmer were so distraught they thought perhaps they were not destined to have children. Once James was born, two years later, they decided not to speak of William. Four years later when Edward was born William was still never spoken of. After Elmer passed, Grandma Mary explained she thought of telling her adult sons of their older brother, but she could never muster the courage. So now a grandchild listened to the regret of a mother who had never shared this secret with her sons.

Mary made some aspects of scaling down her belongings go quite smoothly. After watching several of her friends pass and witnessing the ensuing decision making and arguing about what to do with all the furniture, she formed a plan years ago that was now put into action. On the back of each piece of furniture was taped or tacked a piece of paper stating the name of which relative or family friend would receive this item. Each note was dated and signed. Mary had been working on this project for years. Anytime someone made a comment or indicated interest in an item, as soon as they left the house, Mary would write and attach the note.

As the grandchildren discovered, Grandma Mary was organized and fair in this process. Elizabeth received an Eastlake secretary, dresser, and matching chairs while Mark was given one of the two pineapple-post bed frames along with one of the two matching dressers. "I hope you'll have to wait awhile for the other half," Grandma Mary explained. Nancy received the full dining room set including the china hutch while Jennifer was given the living room...two walnut sofas, coffee table, wing chairs, and side tables. Tommy did not recall ever commenting in a positive manner about one item. So he was a bit mystified receiving the rather dusty, stuffed bird collection, which included the life-sized baby ostrich. But Grandma Mary had also tagged him to receive some lovely office furniture along with two matching seven-foot-tall hall trees with inlaid mirrors.

Mary had been very methodical with the big items. Some of the small items like the yard tools and golf clubs she was not too concerned about, while some seemingly insignificant items she had definite opinions on. She would not explain, but she was insistent that Jennifer receive the cleaning supplies. Grandma Mary was equally demanding that Mark take Grandpa Elmer's collection of now thirty- to fifty-year-old size 12 dress shoes that had no chance of fitting Mark's size 10 feet.

And each grandchild received a clock: a mantel clock, a wall clock, a grandfather clock, an office clock, or an alarm clock. All with one quality in common. They didn't work.

Several weeks into Grandma Mary's stay at Kensington Gardens each grandchild was thrilled to receive an invitation from Grandma to attend a fashion show. Mary Thorpe was going to be a model.

A very savvy local department store had arranged to hold a fashion show in the Grand Lobby of Kensington Gardens. All seniors in the community were invited to attend the show featuring the women of Kensington Gardens modeling a new line of clothing. Fifteen senior lady models were ferried to the store to select multiple outfits to showcase on stage. They were treated like royalty by store employees and informed that any items they chose to model and then purchase would receive a 50% discount. The ladies were also entitled to the same 50% discount on any item modeled during the show. Furthermore, they would receive a 33% discount on any other merchandise they purchased during the week of the fashion show. Smart shopkeeper.

The Grand Lobby, already a beautiful location, was transformed for the event. Comfortable, padded seating for well over two hundred attendees, each chair with a fine view of a slightly elevated runway. High enough off the ground to showcase the ladies and their clothing, but not so high as to make any model dizzy. Even the steps up to the runway were equipped with handrails to ensure the safety of the seniors. Food, drink, and soft background music were all provided by Kensington Gardens staff adding up to create a spectacular event.

Granddaughter Jennifer Taylor wisely brought a camera to capture Grandma Mary's debut walking on stage. Jennifer positioned herself behind the crowd at the apex of the runway to record Grandma Mary's smiling face as she proudly walked directly toward the camera. Unfortunately, Jennifer was so completely stunned by the appearance of her eighty-two-year-old grandmother walking towards her wearing fishnet stockings that Jennifer's camera was instantly lowered to roughly the same position as her bottom jaw. Regaining her composure as Mary was now walking away from her, Jennifer quickly moved along the back side of the crowd in an attempt to get a good shot of Mary's face. Now even with Grandma Mary's position, Jennifer shouted out "Hey Grandma!" Whereupon at least 100 of the 200 heads in the room turned to look at the photographer. However, a second shout of "Mary! Mary Thorpe!" worked much better.

Fifteen senior models move at a surprising good pace. There was no serious delay or uncomfortable pause as one might expect. The organizers had the models grouped in teams of five, so one team was always ready to perform while others were either taking outfits off or putting outfits on. A well-orchestrated event which was as much fun for the models as it was for the audience.

After the grand finale with all fifteen models promenading across the stage at once, Mary was greeted by her grandchildren like The Beatles on The Ed Sullivan Show. Grandma Mary's smile was brilliant as she descended the stairs talking and recounting every detail of the show. Mary's performance on the runway was impressive, but her performance as color commentator was even better. She beamed as she described her dressing assistants who quickly helped her change each ensemble backstage. She raved over her hair stylists who tended and sprayed her hair, being careful not to get any spray on her lovely hats. And she gushed over her beauty assistants who lightly powdered her face while making certain her lips were shiny and her nose was not.

Then Mary led her fan club backstage to her dressing area to pick up her outfits. She had decided to keep four of the five ensembles. The brown tweed coat felt scratchy and was not her color anyway.

With her family in tow carrying the new additions to her wardrobe, Mary led the way out of the main gallery, down the carpeted hall, past the wall sconces to the fifth door on the right side smiling and chattering all the way about the day's events.

Mary Thorpe was home.

Now that fall is in the air and swimming season is over, residents with swimming pools are kindly asked to drain the water off the top of their pool covers. In some parts of town the noise from the croaking frogs is so loud many residents are complaining they can't sleep.

While it is true the problem goes away after the first hard frost of the season, local amphibian enthusiasts remind us it is much kinder to the frog population to remove the standing water before it freezes.

Pool owner John Forrester adds, "The raccoons and jays love the frogscicles and frogpops, but their claws and beaks can damage your cover. Pool covers aren't cheap, so save yourself a few bucks and drain the water."

CHAPTER TEN

Maxine and Fred

If you have not met Maxine Baxter you have really missed out on something special. Maxine is a white-haired, raspy-voiced woman in her mid-eighties with deep, craggy facial lines earned from a good life of hard work. Maxine sounds like she's been smoking cigarettes since she was in the womb, but that would be exaggerating since she's only been smoking for sixty-nine years, a year shy of her seventy years of marriage to Clarence. Though she is a small woman, thin and just over five-feet tall, she is a formidable adversary to anyone who has had the misfortune to be on the opposite side, more specifically the wrong side, of an argument with her. Rumor has it Maxine is responsible for the root words *tank* in cantankerous and *cur* in curmudgeon. That said, everyone who does know Maxine also knows she has a heart of gold and will always help out someone in need.

That generosity was evident to new neighbors Rob and Jennifer Taylor when they moved into the little Craftsman bungalow next door to Maxine and Clarence. Newlyweds, first time homeowners, and only the fourth owners of their antique house, the couple was thrilled to discover solid oak, plank flooring with cherry inlay accents hiding beneath the old brown carpeting. With enthusiastic excitement the yuppies went right to work ripping up carpet, pulling up tack strips, and exposing a well worn, but beautiful original floor.

A pile of debris in the front yard, Rob and Jen would soon learn, is an immediate open invitation to all neighbors to inspect, advise, and criticize whatever project is the cause of the debris. In this case the verdict was distinctly clear. If the neighbor was under forty years of age they loved the wood floor, "You're so lucky! What an incredible find!" While neighbors over forty each knew of a good carpet guy who "Could have this place looking ship-shape in no time at all."

After Maxine saw the floors she went home and came right back dragging two dusty, oval area rugs she retrieved from her garage. Her offer was kind and heartfelt and both Rob and Jen could see the compassion in Maxine's eyes for this poor young couple with the nasty wood floors. When Maxine spotted the wicker chair in the sitting area, that Jen had just proudly purchased at Pier 1 Imports, she offered to bring over an old recliner she had stashed under the house. "The back is ripped and it's got a few stains, but it will do you much better than that rickety wicker," she explained.

Rob and Jennifer learned to listen, respect, and truly enjoy Maxine. Their conversations were lively and frequent though some topics were best avoided because it was apparent that Maxine was always right. Her wisdom was real and her advice, particularly regarding gardening, was sound.

Across the street from both families lived Fred Grayson. Fred was pushing eighty years himself but had only lived in the neighborhood about twenty years so Maxine still considered him to be a newcomer. Fred was a retired machinist who spent thirty years of his life making airplane parts, first for propeller engines, followed by a few years fabricating parts for jet engines.

Though not as brassy as Maxine, Fred was not shy with his opinions either. He was fully capable of telling you why you were using the wrong type of paint and explaining how the President had really mucked up the country at the same time. Fred was just as gray haired and grumpy as Maxine, but he was not as good at it as Maxine was. Watching the two of them in action at the same time looked a bit like a duel in the Old West where one combatant had a shotgun loaded with buckshot, while the other wielded a single shot pellet gun. Fortunately, the two adversaries rarely showed up in the same place at the same time.

To the casual observer it was unclear what caused the tension between the two senior citizens, but the rift was strong and wide. Did Maxine hold it against Fred that his place used to be the local cathouse? No, couldn't be you say. That was over fifty years ago.

Clarence and Maxine never used to lock their front door, until the *second time* an ambulatory, but blurry visioned drunk stumbled into their home looking for some late night action. Just like the first frisky drunk a few months earlier, the inebriated customer did indeed find some action, but not quite the action he hoped for. Before Clarence had a chance to act Maxine was already in action protecting her sons from this deadbeat amorous drunk, bashing him with the business end of a dirty, yellow-handled floor mop. After the second of these incidents, Clarence decided it was time to keep the front door locked at night. Not so much to protect his wife and sons, but more for the safety of any lost, lonely man who might drunkenly stumble in the wrong house on a future night.

All of those late night visits stopped years ago, well before Fred bought the place. Maxine and Clarence kept the door locked every night since then, but surely that was not Fred's fault.

Fred approached Rob and Jennifer one afternoon to discuss a problem he was having with the city. Right about now you should know that Fred was a member of the John Birch Society, so he was always having or ready to discuss a problem with the government. Fred explained the local city fathers had decided to paint the curb in front of the main walkway to his house red, making the space a no parking zone. This was obviously intrusive, he went on, and meant he would either have to park his car in the garage or way down at the other end of his property along the street front. That was a long way to ask an old man to walk with a bag of groceries and, "What business does the city have painting my curb red anyway?"

Fred was canvassing the neighborhood gathering support for his position before going into battle with the City Council at their next meeting. Surprisingly, Rob and Jennifer found themselves in complete agreement with Fred's stance. He sounded very reasonable, made some excellent points, and received assurance from the young couple that they would show up and support him at the meeting.

Sitting in the folding metal chairs in the audience, Jen commented to Rob, "Isn't it great to see Maxine here supporting Fred?" Fortunately for the young couple, Maxine rose to address the council before they were asked to speak. That was the moment, during Maxine's lecture to the council, that the true depth of the Hatfield-McCoy relationship between Maxine and Fred was revealed.

Maxine Baxter was the individual who requested the city paint the curb in front of Fred's house red. Why, you ask? The other side of the coin here is that Fred's preferred parking spot, the proposed red zone in front of the main entry to his house, is located directly opposite of Maxine's driveway. Turns out Fred had been parking his boat length, white over gold Lincoln Continental in that spot on purpose as the position of his vehicle made it near impossible for Maxine to get her white over blue Oldsmobile out of her driveway without maneuvering through a seventeen point turn.

While trying to get out of her driveway, Maxine had even bumped Fred's car several times which ticked off Fred and infuriated Maxine leaving both neighbors more stubborn in their stance of what needed to be done. Both plaintiffs took their turn arguing their case, but even novice attendees at City Council meetings could tell you don't mess with Maxine Baxter. She was the shorter senior, but her voice was meaner and crankier. Of the two she was the one you would not want to meet in a dark alley.

Rob and Jen sat silently watching the show. Wisely neither of them spoke a word and they quietly slipped out the side door as soon as was possible.

City workers came out with red paint the next day. The City Council agreed with Maxine because Maxine was right.

CHAPTER ELEVEN

Barry and his LTBD

If you haven't met Barry Reese yet, now is the time. And if you've only met him once, don't worry you'll see him again.

You see, Barry goes everywhere twice. At least twice. It is not that he likes your company so much, though he is an affable guy, that he can't be without you. Nor does Barry suffer from an obsessive-compulsive disorder where he has to reenter a room and then leave again to ensure he has properly closed the door. Neither is Barry an "Up with People" guy dealing with a case of excessive happiness where every sight and experience the world offers him needs to be replicated to cement it's existence in his memory.

In fact, life would undoubtedly be easier for Barry if he did have one of these afflictions. But alas, life is not easy for Barry Reese as he contends with a seriously life-altering daily condition of.....chronic forgetfulness.

Let's be clear here. We're not talking about "I can't find my watch!" or "Did I remember to close the garage door?" Barry has raised forgetfulness to a lexicographical art form. Norman Rockwell should have painted Barry palm slapping his forehead and then sent the image to Mr. Webster for inclusion in his next dictionary. Barry has a strain of forgetfulness known as chronic LTBD (Leaves Things Behind Disorder).

Anyone who goes out to lunch with Barry knows you'll be returning to the restaurant soon after the completion of your meal. The only question is how long it will take before he or you realizes he has left something behind.

Last week Barry was taking his buddy Rob Taylor out to lunch at one of our finer downtown establishments. Barry and Rob are on an "I'll buy this time, you get the next one" lunch system. When Rob buys the two guys usually end up at a relatively gastronomically tame or boring establishment, like one of those franchised sandwich shops named after underground trains. But when Barry buys the boundaries of culinary delights are expanded to the limits of Rob's delicate digestive system. It's not that Rob doesn't enjoy the taste of unique and exotic foods, but as he has approached middle age he has come to the sad acceptance that his body will no longer tolerate what it once enjoyed.

Kindly, Barry is aware of Rob's epicurean limitations and always makes certain something is on the menu that Rob can eat. Such was the case last week when Barry took Rob to downtown's Old Town Grill.

The Old Town Grill is an amazing little place run by a husband and wife team, John and Debbi. Wonderful folks and master chefs from San Francisco who decided a few years back to leave the big city and treat the folks of our town to some exceptional food. Everything is fresh, hand made, and of top quality. Sure John will grill you a plain burger from grass-fed, free-range beef, but you're more apt to be tempted by his buffalo and elk burgers, bleu cheese waffle fries, or grilled chicken sandwich with asparagus, roasted red peppers, and feta cheese.

At this point you might be thinking that this fare sounds pricey, Barry left his wallet who knows where, and Rob got stuck paying for the meal. Not a bad assumption as that has occurred on numerous occasions, but not last week.

Last week after Rob enjoyed his plain grass-fed, free-range burger and original fries, and Barry polished off his grilled chicken experience and bleu cheese fries, the two friends sat and chatted about life's wonders and mysteries, which meant women. Specifically Barry's women, but more on that another day. The two men were comfortable with their contented stomachs and relaxed with their reclined posture while kicking back and finishing their drinks. As they concluded their conversations, said their thank yous to John and Debbi, and exited the door into the sunny blue skies of Main Street, Barry quickly caught himself remembering he left his sunglasses on the table.

A quick dash back inside the grill, another hello to John behind the counter, and Barry was back outside with his now protected eyes as the two friends walked down the street back to Barry's Subaru. Parking space is often tight downtown. Sometimes you have to walk a few blocks to reach your destination. But generally if the streets are full, you can find a spot, like Barry did, on the second level of the parking garage over by the creek that runs behind the businesses on Main Street.

Now the basic, most direct path from the Old Town Grill to the parking garage takes you across the linoleum tile floor in the Grill, through the cold ceramic tile in the entryway, and then outside onto the concrete sidewalk. At this time of day the north facing Grill on the south side of the street means the sidewalk is in the shade so the concrete is cool. Continuing down the street the texture of the sidewalk changes several times: real wood planks in front of the antique store, bricks in front of the Italian place, and stamped concrete to look and feel like wood planks and bricks in front of the new candy shop. All of this on the cool shady side of the street.

As you approach the crosswalk you drop down to street level on a slope covered with those annoying, hard yellow bumps that indicate to everyone, "Pay attention, you're about to cross a street." As you make your way across the street the black asphalt heats up as you enter the sunshine on the north side of the street. You might also become aware of the undulations in the crosswalk as you walk over alternating patches of asphalt and thickly painted and repainted yellow safety lines.

Continuing on your way to the garage on the north side of Main Street, you find the sidewalk to be of similar construction, but in much worse shape. Due to the greater temperature extremes and more importantly the planting of trees with surface root systems that were much too big for the planting pockets, the north sidewalk has many more cracks, gaps, and upheavals to avoid as you head to the parking garage.

Finally as the stairwell to the garage is in sight you cross four heavily rusted, iron plates covering some old underground access points for several stores and one oversize storm drain grate before reaching the first metal step in the stairwell.

It is at this point, as Barry lifts his foot for the first step, that a glint of reflected sunlight from the ring on the second toe of his right bare foot causes him to realize that he is missing his shoes. Yes, Barry has forgotten his shoes. In the relaxing confines of the Old Town Grill, Barry had kicked back in his chair and kicked off his Birkenstocks.

Leaving behind your shoes and walking barefoot halfway across downtown is not the norm, but it does give you a good idea of Barry's capabilities. More often the effects of LTBD involves Barry's purse.

Yes, Barry carries a purse. Though many have suggested he try calling it a "manbag" or "satchel," it really is a purse. Barry tried referring to his colorful canvas bag with the three-inch-wide shoulder strap as a "murse- the man's purse," for a while, but gave that up after a week or two. Now he just accepts any ribbing he receives and responds with "Yes, I carry a purse."

And good thing for the rest of us that Barry does carry a purse. Leaving behind your shoes in a restaurant doesn't happen all that often. But with all the added space in a purse to carry items around with him, Barry's odds of leaving something behind dramatically increase compared to your average guy who is just carting around a phone, some keys, and a wallet in his pockets. For those of us who know and love Barry, his increased odds of leaving things behind increases our odds of smiling, head shaking, and laughing with our forgetful friend.

The police blotter in the paper reports that seventy-six-year-old local resident Alice Gronewold arrived at Baker's Appliance Outlet last Friday afternoon at 3:06 p.m. in search of a new television. One of those new flat screens everyone is so excited about.

Her husband and passenger George Gronewold, also seventy-six, arrived at the store approximately a quarter second later when Mrs. Gronewold's foot slipped off the brake and onto the gas pedal. The vehicle plowed through the double glass door entryway, traveling through the lawn care and patio furniture sections, eventually coming to a stop directly in front of a row of side-by-side refrigerators.

Upon exiting the vehicle Mr. Gronewold was heard commenting to his wife that they weren't here to look at refrigerators...the television section was over to the right.

No one was injured in the mishap.

CHAPTER TWELVE

EEFSA, LTBD, and Baseball

Unless you suffer from a bad case of forgetfulness yourself, you'll remember our forgetful friend Barry Reese. Barry is the colorful and entertaining guy who suffers from LTBD (Leaves Things Behind Disorder). If you happen to catch Barry around town somewhere you can never be sure if he's out running errands or if he's out retracing his path to all the places he ran errands earlier in the day: wallet in the grocery store, cell phone at the gas station, or shoes, yes shoes, at the local grill. The shoe incident was an earlier story, and probably worth your time, but it won't matter for this story. Just know that Barry can leave anything anywhere.

Those of you who have had the pleasure of Barry's company at your home or workplace either have had Barry back a second time for a quick visit to retrieve something or you're saving an item of his until the next time you see him. Some of us who have Barry in our homes on a regular basis have taken to keeping small baskets, boxes, or bags with a "Barry" tag near our front doors just to make life a little easier for the guy.

Fortunately, Barry is a good man and this LTBD is seen as more of an interesting quirk rather than an annoying quark. But this is not the only interesting trait that is possessed by, or some say, that possesses Barry. Barry is also an EEFSA. Some folks would classify EEFSA as an affliction that requires treatment or at least isolation from the rest of the unsuspecting public, while others, including Barry, look at EEFSA as more of a "cause" to aspire to and follow in your life.

Not familiar with EEFSA? Perhaps you know it by another name, but Barry is an Environmental Education Food Safety Activist. If he'd been born ten years earlier he would be the hippie wearing tye-dye shirts, Birkenstock sandals, and leather bracelets; all while driving a twelve-year-old faded red VW bus with 200k miles on the odometer and peace signs on the back. But Barry is not a hippie. He is an Environmental Education Food Safety Activist. Which in today's terms means he wears tye-dye shirts, Birkenstock sandals, and leather bracelets; all while driving a twelve-year-old faded red Subaru Forester with 200k miles on the odometer and peace signs on the back.

With a heart of gold, Barry is the guy who analyzes your lunch before, during, and after you eat it. He knows the salt and fiber content of the bread you're eating, which bread would be a healthier alternative, and why you should wrap that sandwich in a lettuce leaf instead of bread anyway. And the tuna inside your sandwich can lead to dissertations on fishing techniques and the health of the world's oceans.

Barry can, and will, tell you the protein count of your yogurt and whether the sugars inside are the dreaded "added" type or the preferred milk based. If you're still sitting at the table with him he will further explain the benefits of moving away from cow products and entering the land of goat cheese and soy-based alternatives.

If you are on a hike, picnic, or just at the workplace with Barry, the containers your food has arrived in are also fair game for inspection and review. By now most folks know about BPA-free water bottles and the dangers associated with microwaving plastic containers, but they may not have a clear understanding of the chemical processes involved in how the containers break down and enter your food. If you're not up-to-date on these latest developments in food container safety, after a few meals with Barry you will be soon.

Now the truth of the matter is Barry is right. His commentaries and recommendations as an EEFSA are accurate and above reproach. And anyone who takes the time to try one of his suggestions, whether it be a vitamin-infused marinade for your chicken or a grain with a name that no one can pronounce which promotes a healthy heart, will find that they taste darn good too. Whether we can admit it or not is a different story, but Barry has successfully made quite a few folks around town drop some bad food habits and expand their food choices at the same time.

Depending how you look at him, you might say Barry is not very lucky with love. Or you might be more inclined to say he is very lucky with love, he's just not too lucky with relationships. Barry is never without a girlfriend for very long, but he is also never with a girl for very long. And it is the combination of Barry's EEFSA and LTBD that has contributed to some of his more interesting relationships.

When Marcy, an environmental lawyer who works at the natural food co-op on the weekends, first moved to town, some folks immediately pegged her as a good match for Barry. She was obviously a card-carrying member of the EEFSA society and loved outdoor recreation as much as Barry did. When Marcy showed up at the library for a presentation on composting and then left behind her brown, natural fiber, pea coat at the book checkout counter, folks were positive she was the perfect match for Barry. If she wasn't a true sufferer of LTBD, she had at least given indications that she had a predisposition towards the disorder.

Before Barry and Marcy's first date some of us were already thinking ahead. A honeymoon trip across Europe with lots of outdoor adventures would be appropriate. But a system would need to be devised to ensure the two lovebirds would not leave behind their passports at one of their romantic destinations. And of course they would need to bring along extra pairs of shoes and sunglasses just to be prepared.

Romance seemed to be blooming after their first meeting at the Gelato Deli downtown. Barry ordered a wonderful grilled eggplant panini with red onions and a peach chutney topping, while Marcy had a delicious Mediterranean spinach and chickpea patty topped with tahini sauce served in a whole wheat pita. Conversation flowed easily with topics ranging from whole, fresh foods and the dangers of preservatives to vehicles powered by used vegetable oil and the soiling of Earth's atmosphere. The evening was divine and only made better when after their meal, as they strolled down main street chatting arm in arm, their waiter chased them down from behind to return Barry's wallet and Marcy's coat.

After this success some folks had moved past the wedding plans and were now speculating on whether the couple would remember to bring their first child home from the hospital. But alas, the plans had traveled too far into the future and had not accounted for a surprising revelation.

The second date was an outdoor event. Barry and Marcy planned to take a short day hike and picnic down the road at the state park, but as it turned out, the date might have been better suited to a baseball park.

The pair set out on a pleasantly warm day, just the right temperature to keep a good, brisk pace while walking up and down the trail. Barry and Marcy's ability to hike and converse at the same time was a compliment to their shared level of fitness. As with the first date the conversations were engaging as they walked, talked, and sipped from their BPA-free water bottles. This date was solidly standing on first base.

After an hour they reached the high point on the trail. A beautiful spot surrounded by oaks on three sides with an unobstructed view of the river winding through the small valley below. Here the two fast friends set out their picnic. Barry had brought the blanket, made from organic fibers, while Marcy set out the reusable cloth napkins they would use as plates. Barry opened the bottle of wine made from certified pesticide-free Zinfandel grapes, while Marcy set out the well-worn wooden goblets she used on such occasions. Here the two shared a good laugh and warm smiles as they both realized there would be no food on this picnic. Barry explaining the organic apples and goat cheese were probably in his refrigerator and Marcy sharing her freshly made baguette and Earth-friendly chocolate were most likely on her kitchen counter. This date was now rounding second base on the way to third.

As the shared thoughts and opinions became deeper and more personal, Barry and Marcy realized this relationship might really lead somewhere special. This might be the home run each of them was looking for. They both valued friends, family, and education. They both wanted children and held a desire to travel the world and share those experiences with their children. And most importantly, they each maintained a commitment to using home products that did not emit harmful gasses. Using green certified building materials that stayed well below the volatile organic compound emissions standards was a must in this relationship.

So much in common, so much discovered in such a short time, and so much noise coming from Barry's beating heart, that he did not hear Marcy the first time she made her revelation. Marcy was a switch hitter. But when she repeated the news Barry's heart stopped and he heard her clearly.

Barry knew he and Marcy were both EEFSAs and both dealing with LTBD, perfect for each other is so many ways, but he also knew that he was not ready to join this team. Though he was liberal in life and progressive in thought this was a strike out. Barry knew his male friends would disagree and assure him that a woman who hits from both sides of the plate could be a great development, but he was sure he was not yet ready for the major leagues.

This was a love Barry would have to leave behind.

News item: Locals are advised to avoid Bedford Avenue this coming Friday between the hours of 8:00 a.m. to noon. Traffic will be detoured off of Bedford for several hours as two new power poles are to be set in place.

School board member Tony Lopez announced a generous donation of nineteen large bags of black walnuts at last night's monthly Board meeting. Tony explained the walnuts will be used for counting practice in kindergarten, baking cookies in the middle school home economics class, and interestingly enough, a community relations discussion in the high school government class. The donor wishes to remain anonymous.

CHAPTER THIRTEEN

Maxine and the Walnut Tree

Nobody messes with Maxine Baxter. Or at least anybody who knows of her or heard tell of her is smart enough not to tangle with the eighty-five years of life experience that have made her one of the most ornery and lovable characters in town. Somebody forgot to explain this point to the boys from the power company who came out to prune the branches of her one hundred-year-old black walnut tree away from their electric lines.

The boys first mistake was in assuming that the legal right-of-way laws regarding power lines would apply to Maxine. Workers just showed up the other day and started raising their bucket up into the canopy with the lead trimming guy set to clear a path for the lines just like he had been doing for weeks all over town.

A little background information would be helpful here. You see, during this past particularly harsh winter with heavy winds and record snowfall, lots of folks lost power for extended periods of time. Some people lost power for a few days and others for two weeks or more. And the power outages happened several times due to the wave of storms that continually marched through the area. Anyone without their own personal generator was affected and as you can understandably imagine the situation left everyone upset, irritable, and looking for someone to blame for their lost wages, destroyed food, and damaged electronics. Not to mention the stress, inconvenience, and outright danger many folks had to deal with.

Enter the good people at the power company. Lawyers for the cooperate headquarters had recently lost a sizable lawsuit regarding downed power lines and whose responsibility it was to keep the lines clear of tree growth. Their loss was a tree company's dream as crews were busy all across the state topping and removing trees that had the misfortune of starting life beneath a power line.

Which brings us back to Maxine's front yard. Up in the bucket the trimmer had just pulled the chainsaw to life when Maxine came storming out the front door and down the steps from the porch.

From the first step out the door Maxine started hollering in a voice loud enough to compete with the revving engine of the Husqvarna. Though it might be overstating it to say she was louder than the saw, she certainly held her own in a way that only an eighty-five-year-old voice that has probably been smoking cigarettes for seventy-nine years can.

Nobody actually understood what Maxine was yelling, which was probably just as well. But the general theme seemed to be understood as the saw shut down and the bucket lowered to the ground.

As Maxine was barking at the crew about her property, her tree, and her walnuts, as well as dressing them down about having parked two tires from their "blasted truck on my grass," and how they "better pray they haven't hurt any of the roots to this walnut," this was when they made their second mistake. The wide-eyed, innocent, tree trimming crew chief, who didn't even actually work for the power company, but rather worked for one of the many local tree trimming outfits that had picked up the subcontract to maintain the pathway for the power lines, attempted to explain what was going on.

"Your walnut branches are touching..." he began in earnest before being stared down by Maxine's *don't you dare interrupt me* look.

Of course there was no explanation for this "invasion of privacy, abuse of property rights, disturbing the peace, and destruction of one of the oldest trees in town." While the crew chief was standing there getting his fifteen minute talking to by this five-foot tall, white-haired fireball, that's when another escalation came into play.

Someone, no one has ever claimed responsibility, had called both the power company and the police reporting a loud disturbance on Bedford Avenue. A Sergeant arrived first and upon recognizing Mrs. Baxter stood well off to the side never approaching the angry senior or getting any closer than fifty feet from the offending walnut tree. Tony Lopez, a manager from customer relations at the power company, pulled up next and stepped in to handle the situation. Tony appreciated the "Good luck," comment delivered by the Sergeant as he walked by, but did not understand the reason behind the smirk on the Sergeant's face.

Tony understood the smirk soon enough as Maxine recognized the power company logo on his shirt and turned her lecture away from the crew chief and aimed her barrage at him in mid-sentence without missing a beat or stopping for a breath. Though Tony missed the opening act he quickly learned the plot line as he listened to Maxine bark that this walnut tree was here long before "your blazing power lines" and if that was a problem then "you can damn well move your lines away from my tree."

Mr. Lopez had been on the local school board for several years and was quite used to people sounding off with their opinions on how the world, as well as classrooms, should be run. Those diplomatic listening skills paid off now, as what could have been another mistake was avoided. Tony did not engage

Maxine in conversation, he just listened and nodded his head. Each time he thought Maxine was finished and he could respond, she would start up again about the shade this tree provided and how that shade meant she didn't have to run her swamp cooler all summer which in turn kept her electric bill down. And cutting this tree meant she would have a higher electric bill which is "exactly what you guys want in the first place."

To his credit Tony just continued to listen and nod his head. When he finally did have the chance to interject a comment it was, "You're right." He turned to the beleaguered crew chief and his dazed crew and told them to "Pack it up," and "move on."

But this did not stop Maxine. She kept wailing away at Tony telling him how this walnut tree is "the only thing on this street older than me," and nobody can come in here and "hack up my trees," or even "tell me what I can do with my tree."

"You're right. You're right." Tony kept repeating as he nodded his head.

And Maxine was right.

Some confusion arose in Mrs. Singerman's first grade classroom last week, when for show and tell one student shared he went to a wedding memorial over the weekend. Mrs. Singerman questioned the student, "You must be mistaken. Weddings and memorials are two different events." Nothing was cleared up when the student further explained, "Really, I did! I even got a cool ghost candle for going."

A parent conference has been scheduled for later this week.

CHAPTER FOURTEEN

The Wedding Memorial

An unusual wedding memorial occurred last week. Can you still call it a wedding if no marriage actually took place? Can you call it a memorial if no one died? But before you hear about the wedding memorial you need to know some background about the bride.

Samantha Thompson is a landscaping genius. Everything from vision to implementation is within her realm. Samantha, Sam, can lay the sandstone for a southwestern style patio in the morning and design garden gates for an English cottage in the afternoon. Sam can use the attachments on her tractor to dig twenty-five fence post holes before breakfast, and she'll have the concrete mixed and poured with all twenty-five fence posts set by lunch.

Need a plant? Sam can help you there too. She'll advise you on color, texture, aroma, and how big the plant will be in ten years. She'll even bring in some of her homegrown compost to give your plants a boost.

Sam Thompson is a giant in local landscaping lore. And she is built like it too. Six-foot tall and solid as the rocks she works with, Sam can handle any physical work thrown her way. Her straight, shoulder length, bleached blonde hair, bald eagle tattoos, and imposing physique remind you of the women who stand in a wrestling ring and throw chairs at each other on Saturday night television. She'd also make a great linebacker for the Green Bay Packers. Sam is tough enough to beat the crap out of half the men in town and confident enough to stare down the other half.

But most of all, she's good. Sam works as often as she wants, taking jobs without doing any advertising at all. Folks love her work and know their project will be beautiful.

If you are old enough you might recall an advertising campaign for Sears: "Come see the *softer* side of Sears." Sears was always the place everyone went to buy tools. They had just about every tool invented and if it wasn't in stock they would order the tool for you from their catalog. Plus, with the Craftsman name, the tool was guaranteed for life. Their tools were tough and rugged, just like Sam.

When Sears decided to branch out and get more women shoppers in their stores, someone came up with the *softer* idea. Sheets, towels, clothing...anything else you might want to buy, other than a tool, was softer. Just like Sears, Samantha Thompson had a softer side.

Samantha's softer side dates back to her life before she was the local landscaping giant she is today. Like a lot of little girls, Samantha Thompson loved animals and dreamed of becoming a veterinarian. Unlike many of those little girls, Samantha showed her love by getting a job as a zookeeper's assistant while she was in high school. While other kids went to parties, dances, and football games, Sam cleaned the pens of rhinos, zebras, and giraffes.

As Samantha spent more time cleaning, feeding, and caring for the animals she became more interested in their enclosures. Did the lions have enough space? Did the monkey cage reflect a natural habitat? Are the plants in the tiger area what would be found in their native bioregion? What type of rock would best keep bear claws to the proper length?

And so began Samantha's perfect love affair, combining her affection for animals with her new found fascination with rocks and plants. Four years of college and a degree in Landscape Architecture followed by a state license led to a thriving career doing what she loved. If not for an unfortunate incident in the elephant yard with a constipated pachyderm on what turned out to be her last day at the zoo, two items might be true today. First, Samantha Thompson might be transforming zoo enclosures around the country instead of creating astonishing local landscapes. And second, Sam might not refuse to read any book or view any film involving elephants.

Living on five acres at the edge of town gave Sam plenty of room to store her landscaping equipment. A three-car garage along with a storage barn held trucks, tractors, a ditch witch, various attachments, and loads of hand tools. Years of leftover supplies meant Sam had built up a good warehouse of items for her irrigation, electrical, wood, and rock work needs. Five acres also allowed plenty of room to show off her landscaping talents: limestone patios, slate patios, ponds and waterfalls, stacked granite outdoor fireplaces, and pathways meandering across the property. All surrounded by enough beautiful greenery to make any university arboretum jealous.

Five acres also gave Samantha enough room to house the many animals she dearly loved: one horse, with a sway back and too old to ride, rescued from a neighbor before a trip to the glue factory; a pair of unwanted goats, who turned out to be excellent at reducing tall grass and other fire fuels on the property; and a cat with no eyelids, who was rescued from a university lab, and required eye drops given in the morning and evening.

And five acres was also enough room to indulge in one of her greatest animal loves. Rabbits. Samantha had a soft spot for bunnies. She began with a pair of Dutch rabbits as pets, but soon added a Cinnamon and a Chinchilla. When Samantha found out the county animal shelter only holds rabbits three weeks and if the rabbits are not adopted, then they are euthanized, her rabbit population jumped to a dozen. Throw in a few more rabbits given to her by folks who had an "unruly rabbit" or "this rabbit scratched my kid" and Samantha's warren was over twenty and growing.

Samantha didn't want her rabbits confined to a cage, her rabbits would be free to live a life as open as possible. Rabbits were meant to run, hop, and play in the great outdoors. This desire was the perfect challenge to combine Sam's landscaping expertise with Samantha's passion for bunnies.

Fortunately, that same five acres also gave Samantha enough room to create a bunny paradise. Just off the back side of the house Sam constructed a series of ten adjacent bunny runs. Each run was about twenty-feet long by ten-feet wide and defined by an eight-foot tall, no climb, deer fence. Each run had an outside gate as well as an internal gate so you could walk from one run to the next. Sam had made sure the interior perimeter of the complex was lined with more fencing another foot under ground to prevent escape, while the exterior perimeter was lined with river rock to prevent intrusion from a hopeful coyote or fox.

If rabbits dream while they sleep no bunny ever dreamed of a home like this. Rocks and logs to climb on and under. Bushes to hide in and grass to nibble on. Sunny spots and shady spots. Hard pan soil for running and soft sandy soil for digging. A fresh water creek running through each run. Combine all these features with a daily supply of rabbit chow and fresh greens and you have a bunny ranch that is the envy of rabbits everywhere. But that wasn't everything.

Remember the long, yellow, plastic tubes you connected from cage to cage to let your hamsters play in when you were young? Well, Samantha did not want her bunnies getting too hot, cold, or wet, so she buried ten-inch-diameter drainage pipes from each run to the side of her house. From here each pipe rose above ground and entered her house coming through the wall into ten separate indoor rabbit hutches. Though Samantha could control access to the rabbit tunnels at both ends, most days her bunnies had complete freedom to come and go as they please.

This level of liberty and freedom for all rabbits comes with a price. When you entered Samantha's house your nose immediately recognized the cost. But your eyes were drawn to something other than the wall of rabbit hutches in the family room. Samantha's other animal passion, the skinny, sixteen-inch long mammals that were running around the inside of the house. Ferrets, four of them, had full access privileges to all interior spaces.

Samantha's passion for animals and indifference to animal aromas contributed to a difficulty she had with another mammal. Man.

Samantha Thompson had no trouble meeting men, there were plenty of them around and she was never short of male companionship. But the men she met just never seemed to click. Samantha wanted fireworks in a relationship. While there were several bangs and pops in her attempts at relationships, the oohs and ahhs were lacking. Samantha was nearing forty-five years of age and she wanted the whole show.

Enter Dr. Michael Smith. Samantha met Dr. Mike at a Landscape Show down in San Francisco. She'd attended with the plan of picking up some new design ideas from the big city and spending some time enjoying the wharf and Golden Gate Park while she was there. When Samantha came home she said she met Dr. Mike at a booth while listening to a guy describing the construction techniques involved in building an outdoor earthen oven. Samantha never made it to the wharf or the park, and she never learned how to build an outdoor earthen oven, but she did blush about how much time she spent looking at the ceiling fan in her hotel room. Samantha Thompson was in love.

You should know up front that many of us were suspicious of Dr. Michael Smith right from the start. First, nobody in town had ever met the guy. Second, "Dr. Michael Smith" from "out of town"...are you kidding? But wait, it gets worse.

Dr. Mike was an ER doctor in San Francisco who was always on call and lived at the hospital Sunday night through Thursday afternoon, which Samantha explained meant two things. First, Sam would never be able to reach him directly by phone. She would need to leave a message on his cell. And second, she could only see him Thursday night through Sunday afternoon. Of course this was great with Sam since she worked all day and could arrange her schedule to suit his availability. Because Dr. Mike was on call, he could never venture all the way up to the foothills. The good doctor had to be within an hour's drive of the hospital at all times. Fortunately there was no shortage of hotel rooms within an hour's drive of San Francisco.

Six months of seeing Dr. Mike, and Samantha announced they were getting married. When asked how the proposal happened Samantha was so giddy and bouncy in telling her story you couldn't understand a word she said. No one knew who asked who, or how, or even where the decision was made, but you had to love her enthusiasm. And what of the ring? Sam did make it clear the ring would be a surprise, given to her at the altar.

Which brings us to the wedding memorial. The wedding was set at the Stewart Apple Ranch on the last Saturday in October. Samantha decided on a Halloween theme. The fifty guests were invited to come in costume and celebrate the special day. A dozen circular tables covered with black, white, and orange tablecloths were set among the Red Delicious apple trees while the head table was over by the Gravensteins. Each table had an assortment of miniature witch hats, brooms, and numerous other Halloween items available at any dollar store clearance aisle. Pumpkins and jack o' lanterns were scattered about the orchard and tissue paper ghosts were dangling amongst the golden leaves that remained on the trees.

Darth Vader was conversing with Peter Pan at one table, while Snow White was nursing a bottle of beer and laughing with either Pippi Longstocking or the girl from Wendy's Hamburgers at another. A red-shirted lumberjack was telling jokes to a surfer dude, while a guy who was either an accountant or just dressed as one was in a serious conversation with a guy who was either a computer geek or just dressed as one.

As the Justice of the Peace stepped in front of the head table the guests quieted down just in time to hear Samantha growling, "I'll bet it's that bitch he lives with!" coming from the McIntosh trees.

No one would get to meet Dr. Mike today because the groom was not coming. Peter Pan, Snow White and every other guest began murmuring, squirming, and looking very uncomfortable. After a brief meeting between Samantha, Darth, and the Justice of the Peace, the latter resumed his place in front of the head table announcing there would be no wedding today, but "the bride would like to take this opportunity to share some stories and honor her late mother."

Samantha, in her Elvira Mistress of the Dark wedding gown, stepped forward, thanked everyone for coming and launched into a story about how when her mother died fifteen years ago she could not afford to give her mom a proper memorial service.

As Samantha began her first story about her mother's love for animals and how that had been passed on to her the assembled friends clearly were not sure how to react. When Samantha moved on to a related story about her mother's collection of exotic cat tattoos up and down both arms, the wedding photographer appeared as mystified as everyone else. At the close of this story and through the next several about mom and daughter getting tattoos together, the photographer began circulating through the orchard capturing candid shots of perplexed trick-or-treaters who had come to a wedding, but were attending a wake.

When Samantha began speaking of the many men in her mother's life most guests were now looking down, skyward, or anywhere away from the bride's face. Fortunately, Darth Vader rose and spoke something into Elvira's ear which caused Samantha to stop mid-sentence in her story about mom and a guy named Bill who drove a semi delivering sugar beets to a processing plant in the San Joaquin Valley. With a smile on her face, Samantha changed subjects and proclaimed, "Let's cut the cake!"

Samantha began cutting the wedding, now memorial, sheet cake and placed each piece onto small orange paper plates as she called her friends forward. Like an audition line for a bad Disney horror movie the guests received their cake and offered their condolences to Sam on the loss of her mother. Hugs and smiles were exchanged as folks headed back to their tables and tried to determine if their piece of cake contained part of a witch, goblin, or black cat.

A few in the crowd attempted to slip out of the orchard unnoticed, but were probably glad they were caught and encouraged to stick around, otherwise they would have missed the dancing. With or without Dr. Mike this wedding memorial wasn't finished yet. The Eagles "Witchy Woman" was supposed to be the first slow dance for Samantha and Dr. Mike, but Darth stepped in as Samantha explained this would be a dance in honor of her mother. The theme from *Ghostbusters* was successful at getting everyone out of their chairs as shouts of "Who ya gonna call? Ghostbusters!" rolled through the apple trees.

Samantha and Dr. Mike had burned a CD with an appropriate collection of Halloween favorites which was now being danced to by a happy group of Samantha's friends.

"Monster Mash" was a big hit and easy to move to while the planned big finale of Michael Jackson's "Thriller" was a bust. As much as everyone loved the song, no one in this crowd could lead the group in the classic "Thriller" dance moves. Agreement was reached to just dance any way you felt like and the new finale would be an encore of the *Ghostbusters* theme.

As a tired and sweaty group of trick-or-treaters began to pack up, Samantha made one more announcement encouraging everyone to take home the centerpieces and decorations. Guests left the wedding memorial with pumpkins, witch hats, ghosts, and numerous other Halloween items available at any dollar store clearance aisle.

No one ever got to meet Dr. Mike and he was not missed. However, Sam did set up a time to complete an estimate for the accountant's desire of a used brick patio and Samantha made arrangements to stop by Rapunzel's house and pick up a misbehaving Netherland Dwarf rabbit.

Our City Council claimed Santa Claus as a patriotic American this year, placing the twenty-foot tall, inflatable, red-suited man atop City Hall clutching the rooftop flagpole with the stars and stripes waving proudly above his head.

Several locals complained, not because they resented the implication of Santa as a patriot, but because they thought his particular placement made him look like an exotic pole dancer. The official response from the city was "Hogwash," until Mayor Romano's seven-year-old grandson asked, "Grandpa, what is Santa doing to that flagpole?"

Santa's new home will be next to the community center.

CHAPTER FIFTEEN

Barry and the Missing Chair

As you'll recall, everyone's buddy and all around good guy Barry Reese, has two main afflictions he deals with in his life. First, he is an Environmental Education Food Safety Activist (EEFSA). Though Barry would say this is not an affliction, those of us who know and love Barry are definitely afflicted by his status as an EEFSA. Second, Barry suffers from Leaves Things Behind Disorder (LTBD), a condition that Barry is incapable of denying as half the folks in town have evidence in their homes to prove otherwise.

When Barry walked in to the local school district office looking for an elementary school teaching job twelve years ago, no one on the interview panel knew anything about Barry's association with EEFSA or LTBD. They did immediately recognize that he really did not look the part of an elementary teacher. His long brown hair, pulled tightly against his head in a pony tail that reached halfway down his back only managed to be overshadowed by the light reflecting off the silver and gold earrings on his left ear. Barry had put on a collared shirt and tie for his interview, but the clothing was clearly his "interview outfit." The scene was as incongruous as seeing your classic 1950's high school chemistry teacher wearing longboard surfing shorts and a Grateful Dead t-shirt. Barry looked uncomfortable and the clothes just didn't fit the man.

But there was something about him, an "energy" perhaps that was right. Turns out, he was great with kids too. Hiring Mr. Barry Reese was an excellent decision. He has been a dedicated, exceptional teacher with a tremendous work ethic and sense of creativity that has served the community well for the past twelve years. There was one warning sign at the time, though no one thought anything about it. After Barry's interview the school secretary had to chase him down in the parking lot and return his keys which he had left behind. She found him sitting on the rear bumper of his Subaru changing clothes and sipping from a glass bottle containing some thick, green liquid that she would later learn was liquified kale.

The LTBD is a daily annoyance for Barry, but the guy has come up with lots of coping techniques to "Make it easy to be me," as he says. Lots of people have a spare set of car keys, and some even stash an extra key in one of those hide-a-key boxes under their rear bumper. But Barry adds another layer by having extra keys available at work, with friends, and at two local dining establishments.

Fortunately for Barry he is not materialistic, which makes dealing with LTBD a bit easier. Despite having a successful teaching career and being comfortable with money, Barry doesn't own much in the way of belongings. So when he does leave something behind, the item never seems to be critical to his daily life.

It was Barry's lack of materialism and the rebound from a recent relationship which didn't go where he hoped, that led to another interesting turn in Barry's life. Though Barry has been in many relationships with women over the years, none of them seem to last long. They start out promising, but fizzle out after a few months. His most recent prospect didn't last through the second date, even though the potential was great. Perhaps the despair from that failed potential explains why Barry fell so quickly for the next woman to come along.

Her name was Claire. Their first meeting was innocent enough. They met on the bike trail as Barry was bending over to clean up after his shiba inu and Claire was letting her German shepherd just dump in the middle of a bike lane. In hindsight Barry might recognize that this first meeting was a foreshadowing of what was yet to come or he at least might see this as a metaphor for what was to become their relationship. But no one uses hindsight when they are cleaning up after their dog, though we all might be better off if we did.

No one would look at Claire and deny that she was the earthy type. She dressed the part and did not shave her legs, but she was not a true EEFSA. Claire was a smoker, a drinker, and had no real job. She was a trust-fund kid who became a trust-fund adult. Lots of time to party, but no time to develop a work ethic or even clean her house.

None of Barry's friends could see the connection between the two. Claire ate whole foods and drove a Subaru, but smelled of nicotine and had the thin, weathered appearance of someone who hung out in a bar across the street from the nearest truck stop. This was not a woman who would hike Half Dome in Yosemite, nor would she walk a week on the Pacific Crest Trail. Though she did look more than capable of waiting back at the campsite and helping you celebrate your accomplishments at the end of the trail. Claire seemed to be taking Barry away from his old life and exposing him to something new.

Perhaps Barry was afraid of growing old alone, perhaps Barry was depressed by the failure of his previous relationships, perhaps Barry was lonely, perhaps Barry forgot who he was, perhaps Barry was just an idiot, or perhaps Barry was seduced by someone with no real job who had the spare time to become an expert in the ways of Kama Sutra. None of his friends knew. Barry wasn't talking, Barry was moving.

After just a few weeks of this intense relationship, Barry gave up the lease of his two-bedroom duplex in town and moved in with Claire into her three-bedroom log house about twenty miles south of town.

Naturally Barry's buddy Rob Taylor was on hand to help with the latest of Barry's moves. Of the dozen moves Barry has made over the past fifteen years, Rob hasn't missed one. Fortunately Barry doesn't own much in the way of furniture, but the belongings he does have Rob knows very well. Ten years ago you could load all of Barry's life into a few trips with his Subaru and a couple of loads in Rob's compact car, but now it was easier to rent a small U-haul truck.

Rob considered the weights and weightlifting bench the most annoying items to move. Not because the weights were heavy, but because he knew once he set the weights down in their new home they wouldn't be touched again until the next time Rob showed up to help Barry move.

Barry didn't own a dresser so most of his clothes were in baskets. The grandfather clock wasn't heavy, you just had to remember to remove the pendulum or you would dent the inside of the case. The computer, guitars, and kitchenware were easily cushioned by Barry's collection of southwestern blankets. Thankfully the ping pong table had disappeared several moves back. Barry didn't remember what happened to it, but he also didn't seem too worried about it.

Rob appreciated Barry's wonderful collection of tools which Barry was always willing to share. Each move gave Rob a chance to see what new tool had been added to the collection. The gas powered lawn mower had not yet disappeared though Barry hadn't lived in a place with a lawn in at least the last four moves.

By far the most obnoxious items to move were Barry's *two* refrigerators. Why a single man has two large refrigerators is a story for another day, but just know the explanation involves Barry's qualities as an Environmental Education Food Safety Activist and his Leaves Things Behind Disorder along with a local appliance store's "All Cash Sales Are Final" policy.

Though Barry doesn't own much, his pile has grown with each move. His latest acquisition was a light pine, rectangular dining room table with inlaid, hand painted tiles along with six matching chairs. Barry discovered the table and chairs at a recent neighborhood garage sale and was obviously proud of his purchase as he explained to Rob he was concerned about the tiles breaking during the move. Loading the table right side up as the last item on the truck would ensure it would be the first item off. The chairs were interlaced between the table legs while every inch of wood and tile were covered with pillows, blankets, and clothing from a pair of now empty t-shirt baskets.

With the table secured Rob and Barry headed out to Claire's place. The last quarter mile was a pothole ridden, semi-graveled, dirt road which tested both men's abilities to maneuver their respective car and U-haul around obstacles which, if not avoided, would surely damage both the vehicles and their contents. Approaching the house around a final turn revealed a beautiful, two-story, log house nestled on a slope at the edge of the forest stately overlooking a horse pasture, corral, and barn. Barry stopped the truck thirty yards shy of the house, hopped out, and walked back to the trailing Rob.

"Beautiful isn't it? It belonged to Claire's parents. She got it when they passed," commented Barry lifting open the sliding door on the truck.

"Gorgeous!" agreed Rob noticing the view which inspired the thought of forgetting the unloading and just relaxing on the deck with a beer. "But why are you parked back here? Let's get this rig closer to the front door."

"There isn't room in the house for my stuff, so most of it is going out here in the garage."

"Barry, are you serious?"

"Well, I'm bringing my clothes and guitars inside. And the table is going into the sunroom."

As Barry and Rob carried the table to its new home in the sunroom, Rob asked where Claire was on moving day.

"She went to a wine tasting party," explained Barry.

"At eleven o'clock in the morning?" commented Rob.

"She'll be back late tonight."

Barry gave Rob a tour of the three-bedroom, plus office and sunroom, two-story house. Rob was impressed with the craftsmanship in both the woodworking and stained glass windows. He was equally depressed by the three weeks of dirty dishes scattered around the kitchen and living room. Ants were invading the counters and there were near a dozen bags of trash, beer bottles, and wine bottles waiting to be disposed of. Looking at the bottles it was apparent Claire had an equal taste for beer and wine, but she obviously preferred white wine over red.

Moving on to the bedrooms Rob felt he had to ask the obvious, "Three bedrooms and no room for your stuff? Barry I'm happy for you, but are you sure about this?"

"This will all be fine. The dogs get along great!"

It took about two weeks of living with Claire for Barry to remember he had forgotten who he was. The actual break up was ugly and the two still aren't speaking to each other, so long as nasty emails and texts don't count. Fortunately for Barry, his old duplex was not rented yet. So the following weekend was spent with Rob helping Barry remember what he should not have forgotten...you can't leave behind yourself when moving to a new relationship. Good advice for anyone, but especially for someone who is an Environmental Education Food Safety Activist and suffers from Leaves Things Behind Disorder.

A few months later in his quest to move on with his life and not wait for a female relationship to determine his future, Barry did begin a new relationship...with a house. He purchased his own slice of paradise: a two-story ranch house on a ten-acre spread, perfect for growing organic vegetables, pesticide-free fruit trees, and free-range chickens. The land included a creek and an artesian well, the perfect place for rediscovering yourself and finding the person you left behind.

Of course Rob was the guy to help Barry move and this time he brought along his wife Jennifer. Jennifer was generally right along side Rob whenever Barry was ready to move, but she saw the writing on the wall with Barry's last relationship and refused to have anything to do with showing support for Barry's episode with Claire. Now that Claire was gone Jennifer was back on the moving crew. Good thing too, or else Barry may have never noticed what he had left behind this time.

After the truck was emptied and boxes delivered to various rooms the three person crew began setting up the furnishings: grandfather clock put in place and wound, futon positioned in the living room with a view of the stone fireplace, and clothing baskets arranged at the foot of the bed. A few pictures were hung, while the weights and lawn mower assumed their new stationary positions in a storage shed. The kitchen was unpacked, the refrigerators plugged in, and the light pine, rectangular dining room table with inlaid, hand painted tiles along with five matching chairs were set in place.

"Barry, five chairs for a dinning room set? Didn't you have six chairs?" asked Jennifer.

A quick, but thorough search revealed no sign of the missing chair anywhere in the house or in one of the vehicles. A call to the other half of the old duplex indicated no chair was left behind on the premises.

"Barry, how can you lose a chair?" asked Jennifer knowing full well who she was speaking to and recognizing that was the most rhetorical question she had asked in the last decade. "When was the last time you remember seeing the chair?"

Barry popped open three beers for the crew, sat down in one of his five light pine dining room chairs, and began to ponder the question. In some social situations silence can be awkward and uncomfortable, but this particular silence was patient and instructive. Rob and Jennifer watched with fascination as the victim of Leaves Things Behind Disorder closed his eyes and lifted his right hand. His fist clenched and then opened with a single finger pointing away from his body. If Barry had been conducting an orchestra the pacing and tempo would have alternated from a romantic adagio to an allegro suitable for Metallica.

Barry's mental journey lasted nearly five minutes until the orchestral movement ceased, the eyes opened, and the mouth spoke, "This is going to take some planning. How do you feel about a little road trip?"

Jennifer spoke first upon hearing the plan stating she "wanted nothing to do with this" and she wasn't all that crazy about Rob participating either. Rob had visions of going to jail for stealing a chair, but Barry assured him it wasn't stealing since it really was his chair.

"What about breaking and entering?" asked Rob.

"The sunroom doesn't even have a lock. We're not going to break anything," answered Barry. "It's Saturday night, she won't even be at home."

"Barry, this lady hates you. It's been three months since you broke up and she still sends you flaming emails twice a week. If she catches us sneaking into her house she'll call the cops."

"She might threaten to call them, but I've got an ace in the hole." Neither Rob or Jennifer wanted to hear about the hole card, but Barry showed it anyway. "That sunroom was built after her parents died and she never got a permit from the county. If this gets ugly I've got some good blackmail potential."

"Barry, it's just a chair," pleaded Jennifer.

With Jennifer waiting at home doing some internet research on how you bail someone out of jail, Barry and Rob were driving down a dirt road with their headlights off approaching Claire's house. Barry tucked the Subaru off the road between a pair of ponderosa pines and just behind a large manzanita bush.

The two master criminals approached the house from the upslope side, gaining confidence with each step that no lights were on in the house. With adrenaline running through their bodies, both men made their way down the slope as their feet crunched dried pine needles.

For future criminals or thieves in training, this would be a good point to recognize that wearing sneakers may seem like appropriate footwear when sneaking around, but factually speaking wearing sneakers while sneaking downhill on dried pine needles does not provide you with the most ideal foot traction.

Barry slipped first but took down Rob so quickly that Rob actually finished the slide and hit the back wall of the sunroom slightly before Barry joined him. If either of them was cut or bleeding it was too dark to do anything about it. Rob definitely felt something wet, but couldn't identify the moisture as blood, sweat, or the much more embarrassing result of being scared to death. All three were possibilities.

Stepping over to the deck entryway on the front of the sunroom was now easy even in the dark. There was still no sign of life in the main house so both men turned on their keychain flashlights as they entered the sunroom. Within seconds the accomplices had their lights focused on the same object staring at them in the darkness. But it wasn't the light pine chair.

"Barry how could you leave this behind?" demanded Rob as both men looked at a beautiful oil painting of an aspen grove alongside a marshy meadow. Barry had painted it a few years ago and it had turned out wonderfully. Even in the bright glow of LED flashlights the artwork was impressive.

"We're taking the painting too," ordered Barry which wouldn't have been a big deal except the canvas was stretched over a four-foot by six-foot frame.

"Well, I'm carrying the chair," insisted Rob.

While Barry removed the canvas from the sunroom wall Rob found the light pine chair, but promptly banged something with his shin before he could grab the chair. Again both flashlights illuminated an object in the darkness.

"That would be my coffee table."

"We are not taking the coffee table," insisted Rob.

"It's my coffee table. We're taking the table too," countered Barry.

"Barry, it's a coffee table. The thing is five feet long. It won't even fit in your car. We're not taking the table."

As our heroes walked back to the hidden Subaru with light pine chair and canvas painting in hand they argued about the merits of leaving behind a five-foot by two-foot, eighteen-inch high, wooden coffee table. Rob pointed out to Barry that he leaves things all over town and this was somehow appropriate. If the table is meant to come home it will find its way.

Closing the Subaru's rear hatch, Rob reminded Barry again that you can't leave behind yourself when moving to a new relationship...and a coffee table was a small price to pay to help him remember what he should not have forgotten.

CHAPTER SIXTEEN

Better Rocks and Gardens

If you've ever been out to John Forrester's place on the north side of town you know of his collection of rocks. The guy's property should be the cover feature for every issue of *Better Rocks and Gardens* magazine. John collects rocks like Fat Albert collects calories. John collects rocks like Streisand sings songs. John collects rocks like Madoff misses money. What John had not realized was how this passion would lead him to challenge one of his most fervent moral convictions.

If you ask John how the rock collection got started you might get a story blaming his mother, with John explaining that even his earliest childhood memories involve helping his mom collect rocks from wherever they happened to be. A day trip to the Feather River ended with an ice chest full of tumbled granite sitting in a raft; a week long camping excursion to Grand Canyon brought back boxes of red and brown sandstone in the foot wells of the family station wagon; and a flight to Hawaii Volcanoes National Park returned both 'a'a and pahoehoe lava rocks stuffed inside socks in the family luggage. So when John gives this explanation it is obvious he had no choice, he was destined to be a rock collector.

But other days John might explain his passion for rock collecting by rattling off some one liners about his never-ending need to get stoned. Although those who know John well, understand that need hasn't been a part of his life for twenty years since an unfortunate incident around a campfire involving melting his sneakers to the fire ring rocks while the shoes were still on his feet.

While other days John might give you the more practical explanation that he paid a lot of money for this land and he didn't want any of it lofting up and blowing away in a windstorm. The rock collection was simply a method to hold the earth in place.

Though each of these explanations probably has some truth to them, you should know the land that John so proudly owns was originally gently sloped with not a level spot anywhere on the half acre, and the winds in foothills, though sometimes fierce, have yet to actually carry off an entire plot of land.

Once you have a good look at the rock collection you see it doesn't matter why John collects rocks, but you're glad he does. The guy has a creative side and an eye for making fun and functional spaces out of rocks and plants. Most folks who wander through the gates and pathways feel like they've entered a secret garden combining elements of English, French, and Japanese design. A casual visitor expects to see Mr. Miyagi from *The Karate Kid* emerge from one of the cedar shingled sheds, walk across the redwood bridge over the stream bed lined with river rocks, and welcome you with a warm smile.

Many of the stones John and his lovely wife Rebecca have trucked in are moss rocks that they've used to terrace the land. John and Rebecca have become expert stoners learning to stack and puzzle piece together beautiful stack stone retaining walls held together by patience and gravity without any concrete or mortar. Local landscaping guru Samantha Thompson came out and did the initial tractor work leveling the major areas fifteen years ago, a year after John and Rebecca finished building the house. Samantha, or Sam, delivered the inaugural load of rock and taught the Forresters how to build their first wall. Since that introduction to the art and technique of placing and stacking stones the couple have been on their own. If you see a rock on the property chances are pretty good John or Rebecca selected the spot that rock calls home.

"How many rocks are we talking about?" you ask. After fifteen years the current running total is twenty-eight tons. Yep, that's right, twenty-eight tons. Fifty-six thousand pounds of rock brought in to a secluded, sloped half acre tucked into a quiet neighborhood of single family homes, each on a half-acre to two-acre lot, located about a mile north of downtown.

Friends of the Forresters like to joke about the level of the land dropping in this part of town due to the extra weight placed on the earth, but they do enjoy watching as projects in process become features that are finished. Some folks like helping too. Instead of bringing a bottle of wine to a dinner invitation, they will bring a rock to line a garden pathway. Don't have a gift for Rebecca's birthday? No problem, just bring a nice rock for the yard. But some folks actually liked to help with physical labor.

Our local representative of EEFSA (Environmental Education Food Safety Activist) and LTBD (Leaves Things Behind Disorder) Barry Reese helped John layout the Tuscan Hills limestone pieces for one of the patios in the backyard. Barry was planning on helping cut the pieces as well, but he had to return home and pick up his mallet, chisel, and goggles which he had forgotten in his garage. After the patio was complete Barry and John celebrated with a lunch of deli sandwiches and a lecture on the dangers of sodium nitrate in sandwich meat.

All around good guy, great neighbor, and lovable klutz Walt Peterson has arrived several times over the years to lend his talents as a retired construction engineer. Most recently Walt showed up to haul wheelbarrows full of pea gravel for garden pathways in the backyard, but was given a different job after he dumped a full load of the small, but heavy, pebbles into the fishpond. Walt explained something about a hummingbird being in his way. Of course no one witnessed the hummingbird incident, but we all know Walt well enough to not question the veracity of his story. There were no serious injuries in the mishap though Walt developed some impressive bruises on his shins, and the whereabouts of a friendly koi and two pet store goldfish are currently unknown.

John and Rebecca's new neighbors, the De Luca family, were unsuspecting city folks when they first moved to town, unfamiliar with the lure of collecting rocks. But after a few months of settling in to their own slightly sloped lot, they too became infected with the Forrester's fetish for finding the perfect stone. Helping John layout a bocce court filled with decomposed granite and outlined with lichen covered granite was enough to get Tino De Luca to make a phone call to Samantha Thompson to discuss some tractor work. Though no where near twenty-eight tons of rock at present, Tino and Lisa De Luca have potential to create another gravity well in town as they have almost two acres to fill with rocks.

All of these projects on the Forrester land involve a lot of physical outdoor work and you might expect John and Rebecca to be a pair of muscle bound rock hounds. But you would be wrong. The couple are just your average medium build, middle-class folks who like to spend their weekends landscaping and their vacations hunting for stones.

The results are amazing. In front of the house the moss rock walls hold planter beds filled with a wide variety of Japanese maples, azaleas, and hydrangeas. Along the driveway the leveled beds contain displays of star jasmine, harbour bamboo, and mugo pine. The backyard has the bocce ball area, a horseshoe pit, a fire pit, three sandstone patios, numerous vegetable beds, and of course the recently cleaned fish pond. The plantings in the backyard vary depending on the amount of sunshine each area receives. Purple lilacs, Japanese wisteria, and Baja day lilies take full sun while the Moonbeam hostas, forest grasses, and Maidenhair ferns prefer some shade. Green Globe artichokes love day long sunshine, while the everbearing strawberries prefer some protection from afternoon summer heat. Hundreds of plants and rocks everywhere. John laughs at himself recalling when he started he could identify every plant type on the property, many with the Latin name. But now he pays more attention to color and water consumption rates.

John has overexerted himself a few times. After watching a forklift unload three baskets of moss rock, each basket weighing about a ton, off the back of a semi-trailer and place them in the driveway, John got too excited. He was so motivated to move the rocks to the project area, a new planter bed along side the creek bed, he neglected to pay attention to the most important golden rule in moving stone..."Lift with your legs, not your back."

Midway into the second basket the resulting muscle strain was so painful John stopped working and lay down on the grass to straighten his back only to find his spine was locked in a curled position. Rebecca cracked John looked like a shrimp ready to be thrown on the grill and a few other zingers until she realized he was in serious discomfort.

Helping John into the house, Rebecca tried to make amends for her wise guy remarks with some gentle massage and a soothing bath, complete with bubbles and relaxing pan flute music. John appreciated the attention but still ambled around the house hunched over looking like Dr. Frankenstein's loyal laboratory assistant Igor. Some leftover painkillers from the De Luca family allowed John to walk around in public with reduced pain, but did nothing to improve his posture.

Inability to work, anxiety about an unfinished planter bed, and the monotony of noticing the filthiness of all the hardwood floors in the house conspired to lead John Forrester to a dangerous thought. The mere possibility of the idea caused him pain, so he would not consider following through. He would not even share the thought with Rebecca. Rest. That's all he needed. Rest and the incomprehensible thought would go away.

After a few days of bed rest, ibuprofen, and more help from the De Luca's medicine cabinet provided no relief, John resorted to breaking one of his strongest moral convictions. The desire to stand erect and avoid local commentary on why he walked like a Neanderthal persuaded John he needed help. Pain and curvature in his spine trumped skepticism regarding quackery, which led John to do the unthinkable. He went to a Chiropractor.

Embarrassment, foolery, shysterness...none of it mattered. Desperation leads men to drastic acts. As Rebecca helped John unfold out of the car and shuffle towards Dr. Marcus Gilbert's office door, John noticed the newly painted stripes in the parking lot. In the middle of the lot John realized Rebecca hadn't shaved her legs in awhile, but thought it best not to mention it at this particular moment as Rebecca was supporting most of his weight on this walk. John's stooped spine also gave him a wonderful close up view of Dr. Gilbert's planter beds in front of the office. John's pain was intense but he felt a glimmer of hope as he noticed a beautiful piece of quartzite sitting at the base of a Virdis Laceleaf Japanese Maple.

The nice thing about walking into a Chiropractor's office when your body looks like it is permanently prepared to begin a somersault is the receptionist doesn't ask "What's wrong?" or "How are we feeling today?" John never saw her face that first meeting, but she had a voice like a grandmother about to give her favorite grandson a warm chocolate chip cookie and a tall glass of cold milk. John appreciated her kindness in directly assisting him to the x-ray room before she took him to see Dr. Gilbert in the torture chamber.

While John examined the doctor's light brown, slightly worn out Hush Puppies, Dr. Gilbert gave a brief introductory speech on what the problem was and what could be done. The more the doctor talked the less John listened responding only with "I need some help." Dr. Gilbert continued to speak with John keying in on only a few words. Something about discs, alignment, and vertebrae, but the meaning was lost as John just repeated "I need some help."

Dr. Gilbert instructed John to lay down on the exam table which thankfully was at knee height, so John could just lean down and tip over on to the padded leather table. John winced with discomfort as the doctor continued to pontificate meaningless sounds while he poked, prodded, and hammered at John's legs, hips, and spinal column. As John tried to contain his own sounds to inaudible moans and screams, Dr. Dominatrix positioned John's knees, arms, and shoulders like he was working with modeling clay. The patient was compliant, allowing himself to be molded in any position while occasionally muttering "I need some help."

"You may feel this a bit," was immediately followed by what felt like 227 of Dr. Gilbert's 228 pounds body slamming into John's side. A rush of air and a deep, primordial grunt left John's lungs at the exact moment he heard and felt a bone cracking explosion emanate from his spinal column. In that split second the pressure felt like his eyeballs were being squeezed out of his skull and John was certain he would never walk again. And yet somehow there was a relief of tension that John could feel in his loosened lower jaw.

With no one listening, Dr. Death continued to speak as he helped John up to a sitting and then standing position. As John's hearing began to function again his ears heard they were now going to another table, but his body was focused on something else. Though not standing straight, John realized he no longer looked like the number "7" when he was standing. Dr. Gilbert had a beard and glasses and there were no chains or whips on the exam room walls.

John felt like a wobbly toddler as he walked unaided to the next table. Laying flat on his back was an activity not experienced for a week and though he wasn't comfortable he did feel accomplished. Dr. Gilbert handed John a control pad for the table complete with heat, vibrating massage, and a two piece roller that would lift his back up into the air and press into the muscles on both sides of his spinal column. The doctor advised John that every aspect of this table was adjustable and to go slow at first. John would need to come in every other day for a week or two, but he assured John he would be standing tall before long.

For the first few sessions John referred to this table as the "Altar of Pain" as he increased the height and duration of the roller sessions. Eventually he came to think of the table as a friend who helped improve his posture and ease his pain. John came to wonder how the doctor and receptionist got any work done with this luxurious temptation in the office. A discussion with the grandmotherly receptionist revealed that she enjoyed slipping in for a session with the table on her lunch break and after work.

Much to John's grateful chagrin, his moral convictions about chiropractic care had to change. He began to feel better, almost normal, after a week of treatment. Though he wasn't happy with Dr. Gilbert's command of no rock lifting for two months, memories of pain and wisecracks would assure that John would follow orders. But the doctor's prescription did not stop the passion. The doctor's orders did not specify no rock collecting, just don't pick them up. And the order only applied to John. After all a trip to the grocery store might lead to a find in a parking lot planter bed. Excavation work was being done at the gas station over on Broadway and that might be promising. Even a leisurely walk along the Weber Creek Trail might lead to a unique find. The rocks are out there, just waiting to be found. Which meant Rebecca would have to remember the most important golden rule in moving stone, "Lift with your legs, not your back" or she might be faced with breaking one of her most fervent moral convictions.

The "Green" environmental movement has officially hit the local hospital. A recent patient reports the appearance of biodegradable vomit bags.

Local teacher John Forrester was spotted carrying a plastic bag filled with paper coffee filters in his back pocket. When asked about the filters the non coffee drinker smiled and replied, "I'm working on a project," and quickly walked away.

CHAPTER SEVENTEEN

In Search of the Perfect Stone

Some men spend months looking for the perfect stone. They have met a beautiful woman, fallen in love, and travel to every jewelry store in the state looking for the perfect diamond to express their feelings and hopes for a blissful life together. Others, not yet ready for the altar, but hoping to make a wonderful impression, search for the perfect sapphire, topaz, or garnet to match their sweetie's eyes. Searching for the perfect stone can be a timeless and passionate endeavor.

Fortunately for John Forrester, his wife Rebecca had absolutely no interest in precious stones. She was content with the simple gold bands the two of them picked out together twenty-five years ago. But this truth did not stop John's search for the perfect stone. And how John spent the night of his forty-eighth birthday in the emergency room looking for rocks is a sad tale.

Due to a combination of environment and genetics John Forrester is a rock hound. John, Rebecca, and their renaissance mutt Reni, have been collecting rocks for years. The beneficiary of their pursuit? Their yard.

Call it a hobby, passion, or just good exercise, their rock collection is over twenty-eight tons of stone beautifully positioned around their slightly sloped, lushly landscaped half acre on the north side of town. Their efforts are the envy of the neighborhood, community, and a good portion of the western hemisphere. Landscaping projects are a creative outlet for John and finding a perfect stone is always a satisfying moment.

In John's quest he has looked just about everywhere for stones. He and Rebecca found some wonderful greenish river rocks on a small creek that runs into the McKenzie River up in Oregon. Neither of them had any idea what type of rocks they were, but they agreed the greenish hue would make a wonderful border around a bed of blue iris near one of the blue oaks in the back yard.

John found some interesting blue granite chunks in a future housing development down in the Central Valley. These rocks were about to be buried by a concrete foundation for an upcoming cookie cutter house, so John felt no remorse about rescuing them from the contractor, filling up the footwells of his car, and giving the blue chunks new life as a cairn along the side of Rebecca's prized decomposed granite bocce court.

Last fall John discovered some eye-catching, striped sedimentary stones in a scrap pile behind a new Costco that was under construction. There were enough to fill three of those tough, reusable grocery bags with the cloth handles. Those rocks were stacked in a low, four-inch high wall in the front yard to define a bed of everbearing strawberries.

Some black slate was found along the American River, about ten miles upstream from where James Marshall discovered his rock of choice, gold, back in 1848. Each of these slate pieces was rather heavy, so it took a dozen separate hikes along the trail over the course of a year, at a rate of two pieces of slate per daypack, to gather enough stone to create a bistro size patio area in front of the cedar shingled tool shed out back. That project might have been finished sooner but for the reluctance of all of John and Rebecca's hiking buddies to carry rocks in their daypacks.

Most of the Forrester's projects are done on the weekends with lots of work accomplished on late summer evenings. John tends to work in long stretches, sun up to sun down, occasionally working later than he should. John also is hypoglycemic which in his case means he can't skip meals or else he gets a bit shaky, grumpy, and light-headed. Years ago John discovered that drinking a sugary cola or soda during the work day held off these symptoms and gave him a little extra caffeinated energy to carry him to the end of a project. An additional soda meant he didn't have to stop for lunch so he could move one more rock, dig one more hole, or prune one more tree.

Drinking cola became such a habit that jobs were often calculated in terms of soda consumption. Wiring up the hot tub was a thirty-two ounce cup in an afternoon. Terracing a bed around a newly planted aspen grove would be a two-liter bottle on a Sunday afternoon. Setting up the fruit tree orchard would be a twelve-pack over several days. Removing the shallow spot in the creek bed and straightening out a too sharp curve in the creek would easily require a case of twenty-four cans over a couple of weekends. Of course if the temperature or humidity was higher than forecast on a particular day, estimates for soda consumption would have to be revised.

John's most recent project began on a Saturday morning, his forty-eighth birthday. John had set the day aside to work with Rebecca and finish off a friendly neighbor fence in the front yard. If you are not up to date on what a friendly neighbor fence is, the short answer is your neighbor has some junk, garbage, or debris within your eyesight that you have to look at every day whether you want to or not. Your neighbor has been unresponsive in cleaning up the mess, so you build a fence tall enough to block the offending view, but leave a cute little open space at the top to make the fence less imposing. And of course John and Rebecca would soften the appearance of the fence with a planter bed at the base defined by watermelon sized moss rocks. In total, this project looked to be a weekend project worth about two six-packs of soda.

The Forresters had already set the four-by-four redwood posts in place, so today's task would be to attach the rails, hang the fence planks, carry over the border rocks, and backfill the new planter bed with compost and soil. Fence planks are always put in with screws (nails loosen over time), so the job would most likely roll into Sunday afternoon. The new fence line would measure twenty-four feet with the planter bed extending four feet out from the base of the fence.

John and Rebecca work well as a team and finished eight feet of fence and two sodas for John in less than an hour. Aware of some discomfort in his back, John thought it best to change muscle groups for a while and switch over to moving a few rocks. After the third rock John felt a twinge in his lower back, carefully straightened himself up, and decided to stick with hanging more fence planks. Mindful of his back and unwilling to repeat an earlier adventure at the local chiropractor's office, John washed down a couple of acetaminophen with another soda and continued working, but at a definite reduced pace and upright position. Rebecca attached the planks to the lower rail while John worked the upper rail. This routine worked well as the partners completed another eight-foot section, though the time for completion was roughly double the first section, with the same two-soda allotment.

John's back was tight but the pair stayed with the job and completed a good looking, twenty-four-foot redwood fence by early afternoon with John consuming a total of seven cans of soda and a second dosage of acetaminophen. The six-inch window detail at the top of the friendly neighbor fence gave the structure a Craftsman's era touch that was an attractive and practical addition to the yard.

With plans for a birthday dinner and a movie, John and Rebecca decided to save the remaining rock and soil work for another day. Tonight would feature a delicious meal of New York steak, fresh green beans, mashed potatoes, and garden salad with a bottle of Syrah. Then some popcorn and curling up on the couch to watch a DVD of *The Family Stone* which everyone in town said was a wonderful film and they couldn't believe the Forresters had not seen.

Not finding much relief from the acetaminophen, John had popped a couple of ibuprofen before dinner. Between the pills and Syrah John was feeling comfortable again by the end of the meal. Halfway through the film though, John got restless and had to give up his birthday cuddling with his wife. Pacing behind the couch, John alternated between watching the film, touching the back of Rebecca's head, and encouraging his beloved mutt Reni to lie down and stop following him as he attempted to walk off his sore back.

As it became more evident a character in the movie wasn't going to make it to the end of the film, it became more evident to John he wasn't going to make it to the end of the film either. John's pacing became pacing with moaning. Pacing and moaning became outright pain. Outright pain became take your breath away what the hell is going on? John didn't know what was happening, but he knew this wasn't a chiropractic problem. As he doubled over to the floor with Reni licking his face, John called to Rebecca, "We're going to the ER."

Wrapped in the movie Rebecca replied, "No, I think they'll call Hospice."

"No, we're going to the ER. You are driving me now!" which got Rebecca's attention as she grabbed the car keys and helped John hobble into the backseat.

Living five minutes from the hospital was never more appreciated by both the Forresters as Rebecca was guessing appendicitis while John's moaning was now punctuated with swearing and not so polite requests for help with the pain.

Emergency rooms can be frustrating places with long lines, wait times, and ridiculous questions, but when John wobbled in at eleven o'clock on a Saturday night to find no patients at all, he would later look at this as a generous birthday gift. The staff whisked him away while Rebecca took care of the details at the desk. Laying on a gurney John was sure his grip on the side rails had left an impression in the metal.

"My gut, my back, my sides!" was John's answer to the obvious questions while he was writhing on the bed. "Let me stand up. No, I need to lie down. Let me try sitting," rattled out of John's mouth as a nurse put in an IV line.

Blood tests take forever when you are in pain, but when the pain is agonizing time seems to move even slower. After what John said was an hour but Rebecca assured him was only a few minutes, the okay was given to administer drugs. The initial round of pain meds delivered through the IV had no effect on the pain, but they did make John nauseous as the first round of emptying his stomach barely made it into a nearby trash can.

For the contents of round two a nurse handed John a green vomit bag with a triangle made out of black arrows printed on the side. John and Rebecca would later comment how nice it was to know our local hospital was using biodegradable materials in the ER. Anti-nausea medication was added to the IV along with another dose of morphine. By the fourth dose of both meds John could lay still on the gurney and the moaning ceased.

With John now relatively calm, semi-coherent, and fully medicated, he was rolled down the hall where an MRI and ultrasound revealed he was the not so proud owner of a quarry of kidney stones. The doctor explained the *first* stone was well on its way to freedom and might pass in an hour or so, but the remaining three stones might take several days to complete their journey. And sometimes one stone may break apart into several along the way.

"Passing these stones can be very painful, the process is known as the male version of childbirth," continued the would-be obstetrician. "The best thing you can do is stay medicated, drink lots of water, and filter your urine."

"Filter my pee?" asked John.

"Yes," said the doctor as he handed John a cone shaped item made from what appeared to be plastic mesh. "You'll need to urinate through this filter so you can capture some of these stones. Then we can analyze the stone and determine what may have caused them. Some kidney stones can be prevented."

"You mean I can stop this from happening again?" John asked in a desperate yet hopeful voice.

"Once you've had kidney stones you're more apt to get them again," said the doctor, "but you can help yourself."

"And how do I do that?"

"Do you drink much soda pop?"

The first day of filtering urine had moments of excitement as John felt he was at a county fair shooting a semi-automatic rifle at a yellow duck target. The weapon would jam on occasion, but feel wonderful when firing resumed. However, no stones were recovered on day one. Whatever had come down the pipe had broken up into pieces too small for the mesh to capture. The search continued.

By the middle of day two, the hospital issued filter was understandably incapable of further use, so John switched over to Rebecca's Melita No. 4 size coffee filters. They filtered well but John discovered he needed to start and stop his urine flow so as not to overwhelm filter capacity. Apparently the flow rates of human urine vs. hot water from a Gevalia automatic drip coffee maker were not equivalent and a possible topic for future investigation.

On the evening of day two Rebecca reported hearing a shout of joy echoing from the bathroom like John had just won the lottery...the big, super, mega, multistate, multinational, intergalactic lottery.

"Rebecca, get in here. You have got to see this!" is not a phrase anyone generally shouts from the bathroom. Nor is it a phrase that would generally garner enough interest for anyone to enter the bathroom. But Rebecca was supportive and a rock hound herself, so she excitedly joined her husband who was now dancing in front of the commode.

Sitting at the bottom of a now damp and formerly white coffee filter was a jagged, straw colored, harbinger of death. The stone looked like the destructive crystalline entity from an episode of *Star Trek* (the one without William Shatner). Close examination revealed edges appearing more jagged than the Swiss Alps and Grand Tetons combined. John said it looked like "a collection of steak knives bound at the handles with the serrated blades pointing in all directions creating an orb of doom."

The stone measured three-millimeters in diameter which doesn't sound like much until you consider the narrow path and the specific location of the narrow path the mighty entity traveled. John was elated. He spoke of mounting the stone on a ring. He could encase his creation in a lucite cube. John's pride and relief was only broken by Rebecca's pass on the offer of a ring and her reminder that "there could be three more."

And the search for the perfect stone continues.

Officials at the high school threatened to cancel next month's annual Homecoming Dance and Football game after it was discovered the student body's selection of the English rock band Queen's "Another One Bites the Dust," as the homecoming theme did not refer to the strength of our football program and how we would win the contest. Rather, the selection was meant to not so subtly point out our current streak of losing the Homecoming game for seven years in a row.

The dance and game were allowed to proceed after a compromise was reached. All offending buttons and banners will be replaced and the student body has selected a new Homecoming theme, "When You Wish Upon a Star."

CHAPTER EIGHTEEN

Rock Hound

Any story with a dog in it never ends well for the dog, and this story is no different. But for the faint of heart and members of the local Society for the Prevention of Cruelty to Animals, you should know the dog survived and is happily jamming his nose inside an empty peanut butter jar, creamy style Skippy, attempting to reach the last remnants of treasure with his tongue that were unreachable with a kitchen utensil. With that knowledge secured, perhaps you will be more comfortable hearing about the incident involving John and Rebecca Forrester's dog Reni.

As you know by now John Forrester is a rock hound. John and his wife Rebecca collect rocks from anywhere and place them in beautiful landscape creations on their slightly sloped half acre on the north side of town. Pea gravel pathways lead visitors through terraced gardens defined by moss rock retaining walls. Redwood bridges cross over river rock stream beds. Sandstone patios surround a cozy fire pit and dining areas. Sheds with cedar shingle siding contain the shovels and tools used to bring in the twenty-eight tons of stone and hundreds of plants used in the property so far.

John and Rebecca have carefully selected and placed nearly every rock and plant in its current location. Some items have been placed and replaced in their location more than once thanks to the assistance of the Forrester's faithful apprentice Reni.

Reni was added to the Forrester family twelve years ago when John and Rebecca came out of the grocery store carrying a bag containing soda pop, peanut butter, bananas, and wheat sandwich bread. If the bag had contained milk, ice cream, or anything that needed to stay cold, John and Rebecca never would have stopped to look at the four puppies in a box marked free.

Rebecca had always wanted a frisbee dog. One of those graceful, agile dogs that darts across the grass, leaps into the air, and with a twisting body grabs the frisbee in mid-flight. Then the beautiful dog races back to his owner and jumps into his master's arms ready for another toss. When the lady behind the box said the mom was "some kind of a cross between a border collie and an australian shepherd," Rebecca's ears perked up. When the lady continued they thought the dad looked like a "cross between a golden retriever and a terrier," that was more difficult to picture, but Rebecca was sold. The sandwich supplies were put in the back seat and Reni, short for Renaissance Mutt, rode home in Rebecca's lap.

Reni's tenure as a frisbee dog was short lived as he was terrific at the racing and catching part, but more interested in eating the flying disk than returning it to his master. But Reni did play a helpful role in the Forrester family. Reni became a true rock hound, every bit as dedicated as John and Rebecca.

Of the twenty-eight tons of stone moved onto the property Reni could claim several hundred pounds of those as his contribution to the landscaping. Reni was accomplished at carrying mouth-sized rocks from point A to point B which made him a helpful and valued member of the team. Though occasional artistic differences arose as Reni moved or removed stones which he felt had not been placed in an aesthetically pleasing position.

Most of the artistic squabbles were inconsequential with the exception of a two-month period after Walt Peterson had come to help with a project. Walt had somehow accidentally dumped a wheel barrel full of pea gravel into the fish pond and Reni must have been observing. That was the only explanation for the start of Reni's daily habit of dropping rocks into the pond. Watching a dog drop stones into a fish pond and try to catch the resulting splash in his mouth is entertaining at first, but not particularly helpful to the local fish population. Several weeks of intensive training broke Reni's habit, but did nothing to cure Walt Peterson of his legendary klutziness.

Walt Peterson and Barry Reese came over to the Forrester's place to help finish up a recent project. John and Rebecca had built a gorgeous redwood trellis above a limestone patio dining area and were ready to add some lighting. This would require moving some rocks, digging a trench, and laying some conduit to the site before pulling wire, connecting the three overhead lights, and adding a GFCI outlet at the base of one post.

Naturally Barry forgot his tools, which you might think was just a ploy to avoid helping with the trenching. But Barry is famous for his forgetfulness so a quick trip back to his place wasn't a surprise. Anyway, a trip back home would allow him to pick up the other item he forgot, his dog, a six-year-old shiba inu named Pat. Since Walt had brought his dog, an eight-year-old golden retriever named Jake, the plan was the three dogs could play together while the three men worked together.

As Barry left, Walt and John headed out to pick up the trencher at the rental shop. The shop manager, Gary, knew both Walt and John well making sure that John sign for the optional insurance rider if he planned on letting Walt behind the controls. Ever since the incident involving Walt, a flying body, and a formerly functioning post hole digger, Gary was insistent on Walt getting the "optional" insurance. Gary reminded the boys this was a powerful machine and to take it easy on the throttle when moving it around. As they powered up the the trencher's engine to drive it up the ramp into the back of Walt's pickup, John wisely offered to take the controls of the beast so Walt wouldn't lose another rear window as he did during the wood chipper incident last winter.

Leaving the rental shop Walt made a quick stop across the street at the Hangtown Brewery and Tasting Room. Amazing how someone could put a brewery right across the street from a place where you can rent nearly any type of mechanical device capable of maiming the human body in unimaginable fashion, but there it is. Walt assured John that his purchases would be for consumption after the workday was complete.

Back at the house a six-pack each of ale and stout were set to cool in the fridge while the work began. Unloading the trencher wasn't a difficult process, but it wasn't helped by the presence of three dogs one of which thought it was great fun to run up and down the ramp while the machine was backing down said ramp. With the moving of a few stones in a retaining wall and clearing pea gravel from a pathway, John set the trencher in action, easily clawing through sod, pathway, and planter bed to a depth of twelve inches. So easily in fact John wondered why he had rented this beast, but reminded himself that trenching the thirty-two feet by hand to the proper depth would have taken most of the day. Besides, if they had trenched by hand Walt would have easily broken more than just the one sprinkler line John broke.

While Barry hooked up the circuit breaker John and Walt lay conduit and began pulling wire. Alongside the men, Pat was yipping and trying to reach the breakers while Jake and Reni were in charge of simultaneously digging new trenches and dragging the conduit to where they thought the pipes should be placed. They were quite a team and despite working against each other the six companions worked productively toward their goal throughout the afternoon.

Walt and John managed to hang all three lights from the trellis while Barry was connecting the switch and outlet along with running wire to each light. Now that the three men were each up on their own ladder their three counterparts played a less vital role in helping, preferring to curl up at the base of their master's ladder towards the end of a long day.

Approaching the dinner hour the boys wanted to test out at least one of the overhead lights before taking a food break. The last step was to connect each light and turn on the power. Three lights, three guys. Each man would get the honor of hooking up a light and testing it out. Walt, being the oldest, would get the first light. Twisting on his three wire connectors, placing the cover on the junction box, and screwing in the light bulb all went fine so Barry went to turn on the circuit breaker. John flipped the light switch and....let there be light! This went so quickly Barry wanted to take his turn and hook up the second light fixture. Walt unscrewed the bulb from the first fixture for Barry to use in the second, John turned off the breaker, and Barry twisted his connectors, covered his box, and screwed in the bulb. John hit the breaker on, Walt flipped the switch and...voila! Illumination!

With grumbling stomachs, the three workmen unscrewed the lightbulb, roused their companions from the base of each ladder, and headed to the house for a bite to eat. John's light would finish the day and provide a warm glow to enjoy an evening beer and admire their work as the sun dipped below the horizon.

Pat, Jake, and Reni perked up on the way back to the house, perhaps hoping their evening meal might include more than a bowl full of kibble. The canine trio was not disappointed. As the men chowed down on barbecue steak, potato salad, baked beans, corn on the cob, and sourdough bread each faithful companion received some tasty treats from the table. The longer the meal progressed the more generous the handouts from master to grateful beast.

Pat and Jake may have been accustomed to success at begging at the table, but Reni was not used to this good fortune. Perhaps it was because guests were visiting or perhaps it was because the first six-pack of Hangtown beer was opened and consumed with dinner, Reni didn't care. This dog was living large: patiently accepting treats from John and then casually muscling in on Jake's territory swiping treats off the floor. Barry didn't seem to notice the height of his dog had changed as the taller Reni took scraps from his hand before Pat ever had a chance. Barry's absent-minded pat on his new taller dog's head just kept telling Reni this was the best day of his life.

If humans can tell stories about great meals and the impact on their lives then dogs should have the same right. And Reni was living a story for the ages. Being your typical dog, Reni has no off switch when it comes to food so he just kept up the pace through the entire meal, even cleaning up a dropped fork and consuming a paper napkin covered with melted butter and remnants of hickory smoke barbecue sauce.

As plates were cleared and chairs pushed in, John noticed Reni seemed a bit bigger in the belly and gave his contented buddy a congratulatory scratch on the head as three men and three companions aimed back to the redwood trellis and the awaiting final light fixture.

In the darkening skies John ascended the ladder to complete the final task of a long day's work. Walt and Barry held opposite sides of the ladder while shining flashlights on the overhead junction box. Reni assumed his position at the base of the ladder curling up against the ladder legs and instantly fell asleep in what appeared to be a food induced coma. Pat and Jake settled in near the feet of their respective masters.

John was about to twist the first wire connector, but needed to strip off some covering and expose more wire to make a solid connection. As John clamped down on the wire a fountain of sparks burst into the sky like the bicentennial Fourth of July celebration in Philadelphia. The flash of light lit up the entire yard like lightning fills the sky from an approaching thunderstorm. And the accompanying sounds were astounding. The buzz of electrical discharge was first, but which sound came next was difficult for all to discern. Was it the screams of three men? Maybe the wire strippers and flashlights hitting the patio? Or perhaps it was the lightbulb exploding as it hit the stone? Whatever the order, these sounds were immediately followed by the yelping of two dogs quickly followed by their toenails scraping on limestone as they escaped the shower of sparks.

The pain in John's left shoulder from falling off the ladder and landing on limestone was overshadowed by the buzzing and numbness in his hands, right arm, shoulder, and leg. Sprawled on the ground John was relieved he had not landed on Walt, Barry, or any of the dogs. As Walt and Barry knelt down to help, John's eyes focused on the motionless dog at the base of the ladder. Reni was not moving.

With his numb hands John touched Reni's head and belly. Reni was not breathing. Reni's eyes were closed and his mouth was open with his lifeless tongue laying on the stone. John looked at Walt and Barry saying "No, it's not time yet." John slid Reni's tongue back inside his mouth, held it closed, and began mouth to muzzle breaths. Puffing air through his buddy's nose John could see Reni's belly rise. Walt wasn't sure exactly where to press, but began chest compressions on either side of Reni's right shoulder.

What seemed like hours was probably less than two minutes of breathing and pumping until Reni lifted his head and began licking his master's face.

Though Walt explained he had been shocked numerous times himself over the years, beginning with a science experiment involving a fork in his kitchen when he was a kid, he assured John that he would be numb for a while, but he would be fine. As for Reni, Walt continued, he didn't know. Walt had never been knocked lifeless and he had no experience with dogs getting shocked so this was out of his area of accident expertise.

"Let's get him to the vet," John stated as he cradled Reni and carried him to Walt's truck. As Walt drove the ten minutes to the animal hospital John was worried both by Reni's lethargy, there was none of Reni's usual interest in sticking his head out the window, and by the clumps of fur coming off Reni's body as John gently pet his head and belly trying to comfort his companion.

Having received Barry's phone call, Dr. Slate wasted no time and began examining Reni as John was carrying him into the exam room. John was appreciative it was Doc Slate's turn for the late shift on a Saturday night. The Doc loved all animals, but she always seemed to have a soft spot for Reni, and Reni seemed to feel the same. Doc didn't question John as he set Reni on the floor rather than the exam table as they both knew Reni's dislike of the stainless steel table.

Doc checked Reni's breathing, heart rate, body carriage, joints, skin, eyes, ears, nose, toenails, and teeth. Reni was so still and compliant he received the most thorough physical he'd ever had in all his twelve years. Finally Doc Slate turned to John announcing Reni would be fine. Her only negative comment was about Reni's ground down teeth, but she wasn't serious. Doc Slate had stopped admonishing Reni and John about chewing on rocks six years ago. Doc explained Reni was apt to be sore for awhile and he would probably end up with some bald spots, but he didn't suffer any serious electrical burns or other damage. Her prescription for Reni was to "Take him home, keep an eye on him, and call me if anything comes up."

However, Doc Slate did have a prescription for John. During Reni's exam she couldn't help notice that John's fingers and palms were both bright red and swollen. Doc said these were minor burns and coated the areas with an antibiotic ointment and wrapped them with gauze. She was laughing as she told John "I always advise my patients not to lick their wounds and I generally put one of these around their neck," and wrapped a plastic cone, around John's neck.

Doc was still laughing as she turned to Walt saying, "Take him home, keep an eye on him, and call me if anything comes up."

Due to a high volume of calls to pick up misbehaving pet rabbits, local animal rescuer Samantha Thompson is offering the first in a series of "Better Bunny" classes this Saturday.

Workshop participants will be guided through the steps on "How to build a positive relationship with your rabbit." Litter box training and anti-chewing strategies will be discussed at the first class. Ms. Thompson promises rehabilitating your rabbit is possible.

CHAPTER NINETEEN

Ribs and Redemption at Mostly Franks

Last time Rob Taylor chose the food for the annual viewing of the USC vs. Notre Dame football game his food selection inadvertently led to a divorce. The failed marriage wasn't his own. Rob and Jennifer were doing just fine. The rift was in Danny and Laura Halton's relationship, and Rob's choice of the guys going to watch the game at Marco's Cantina ripped the rift wide open.

Usually the guys, which consisted of Rob, Danny, John Forrester, Walt Peterson, along with occasional drop-ins, would gather Saturday afternoon at one of their houses for a long afternoon and evening of chips, beer, and various types of food. Sometimes the group would plan a barbecue while other games were more of a potluck. Generally the food selection was fine and if it wasn't, a slight increase in beer consumption made sure no one cared.

These gatherings happened about once a month, depending on the quality of game and everyone's schedules. A successful routine like this obviously involved keeping the wives and families happy, which was easy. None of the women were anti-football, in fact they were all well versed in the game. But the women all shared a common love of literature. So while the men were getting their football fix in one house, the ladies held their monthly book club in another.

While attendance at some games was flexible, the annual USC-Notre Dame matchup was mandatory. A game of this magnitude required more than just the usual fare, so the guys would alternate planning the food. Which brings us to four seasons ago when Rob last planned the meal and his fateful decision to "do something different this year."

Marco's Cantina would be the scene for the big game. A full taco and burrito bar, lots of imported beer, high definition televisions, and a loud crowd to pump up the atmosphere. Our boys were all having a grand time, but the crowd was apparently having too much fun. During the second quarter Marco himself announced the crowd was getting out of hand, there was damage to the bathroom, and if they didn't take it down a notch he would call the cops. That admonishment was enough to calm down the voices of our four friends, who really didn't think they were part of the problem anyway.

Apparently the lowered volume of the crowd wasn't enough to satisfy Marco as two officers showed up just as the first half closed. The male and female partners stepped right in front of the biggest screen as Marco shut down all the televisions in the place. Any uniformed officer commands respect and this woman was no different. The entire cantina went silent as she lectured the crowd on noise level and destruction of property. She cited several code violations and rattled off infraction code numbers as grown men around the room hung their heads in shame. At the close of her lecture she threatened to bust up the crowd if they didn't knock it off, and with the words "bust up" the officer ripped off her uniform shirt exposing the type of bust she had in mind. An arresting pair of double D's minimally covered by a pair of hot pink, fabric triangles roughly the size of two tortilla chips sitting on the boys' table.

The officer's noticeably muscular partner immediately stepped aside and turned on some classic bump and grind music while the main attraction tore off her uniform pants revealing two additional hot pink, fabric triangles doing their job below the equator. The dance moves were impressive and Rob couldn't ever recall such a fascinating halftime show.

Once the show and the game were over and his head clear, Rob headed home and immediately shared the adventure with Jennifer. Rob recounted all the details, particularly laughing at himself for how naive he was. Jen got a kick out of the story too. So much so that she repeated the story at the next book club. Reaction was mixed. John's wife, Rebecca, laughed with Jen as she had heard the same story right after the game last month. Though she had heard the C cup version. Walt's spouse, Barb, had heard the tale as well. Barb wasn't offended, and was really more embarrassed than shocked. But Danny's wife, Laura, was silent. Her lips pursed, face tightened, and skin flushed...the woman was ticked. Apparently Danny never shared the story with Laura and it wasn't the first time. The separation was immediate and divorce followed quickly.

With that experience in his background Rob, right or wrong, had always felt some guilt and responsibility for Danny and Laura's split. The divorce was ugly. Laura had moved out of state and Danny had ostracized himself from the group. If Rob hadn't told his wife maybe none of this would have happened. Rob was reminded of this thought at every football game, but particularly at the annual USC-Notre Dame classic. Which is why Rob refused to organize the food for the big game, he wanted no more responsibility for failed marriages.

Which brings us to this year's game when John, Walt, and new member Barry Reese insisted that Rob plan the feast. Reluctantly Rob agreed, but insisted Marco's was out of the question as was any Mexican food. For that matter, they wouldn't be going out at all. Rob declared the game would be shown at Walt's house and Rob would bring the food. Rob would select something completely different that none of them had done before.

Rob needed advice on the best take out in town and he knew just who to ask. Ask the one person who is always right, his cantankerous, yet lovable, eighty-five-year-old neighbor Maxine Baxter. Maxine has been around town longer than just about anybody, except her ninety-four-year-old husband Clarence, and she is an authority on everything. If you don't believe it just ask her and she'll set you straight.

Before Rob had explained the whole premise, Maxine interrupted with, "You like ribs?"

"Sure, where's the best place for take out ribs?"

"You want Mostly Franks and no, they don't sell hot dogs. It's a bar that sells barbecue ribs. You're not going to want to bring Jennifer in there, just call ahead and they'll have your food ready for you. He's on the highway just south of town, down past the taxidermy place."

Maxine spoke with her usual straight talk, no nonsense voice and Rob was sold. He made the call Saturday afternoon and was surprised by the ordering system. You ordered your ribs by the pound at $9.00 per pound. Each pound of barbecue ribs got you a carton of slaw and some bread. That's how it worked, no substitutions, no special requests, no exceptions. Take it or leave it. The guy on the phone wasn't rude, just matter of fact. He didn't care whether you ordered ribs or not, but with his "What's it gonna be?" statement it was obvious he wasn't interested in small talk.

Being out of his element with the ordering system, yet not wanting to ask how many people one pound of ribs would feed, Rob decided to play it safe and figured ten pounds would be enough for four, friendly, football fans.

"What time?"

"Pardon?" asked Rob.

"When do you want to pick 'em up?"

"Does four o'clock work for you?"

"Ten pounds. Four o'clock. Cash only," stated the man, not giving Rob a chance to continue the conversation.

As Rob parked in the empty lot next door to Mostly Franks he realized he had passed this place a hundred times and never given it much thought. Mostly Franks was an old cut stone and brick building with no windows on the front or the side facing the parking lot. The entire outside wall of the building had been painted with an advertisement for a beer that Rob had never heard of. From the condition of the painting, he guessed no one else in the last forty years had heard of that beer either. A small, two-sided, neon sign buzzing the name Mostly Franks precariously hung above the metal front door. Rob felt out of place as he walked up to the entry. A large man with his arms folded across his sizable chest blocked the doorway stating, "What do you want?" The words were more of an accusation rather than a greeting.

"I'm here to pick up some ribs?" replied Rob feeling rather small next to this behemoth.

"Go 'round the corner," he said with his arms still folded but lifting a single finger pointing to the far side of the building. "First door you see."

Rob walked around the corner into a long alley. This side of the building had the remnants of another unknown beer advertisement painted sometime during the last century. Along the left side of the alley was a long row of mixed bushes and trees. Rob noticed there were no special varietals in this mix of plants, nothing John Forrester would put on his property. This was a solid wall of evergreen plants meant either to prevent alley walkers from seeing what was next door, or more likely to prevent whatever was next door from viewing the activities going on in the alley.

With Rob's first steps into the alley movie scenes came to his mind. Robert Redford from *Three Days of the Condor* would be looking to meet his old buddy in this alley and then find himself dodging bullets and diving behind metal trash cans just as his buddy gets plugged in the forehead by an assassin's bullet.

The hairs on the back of Rob's neck began to rise with another step and another movie entering his mind. Redford again, but this time he's with Paul Newman. Sundance is providing cover for Butch Cassidy as the two are creeping their way through some village side street unknowingly trying to evade the Bolivian army. But Rob realizes he has no partner. He is walking this alley alone.

Another step, another movie. This time the silhouette of Clint Eastwood is standing ahead at the far end of the alley. Clint's shape and words alternate from Dirty Harry saying, "Go ahead, make my day," to that Spaghetti Western Rob could never remember the title of where old west Clint outdraws several sweat-faced bad guys at the same time. Rob knew Clint wasn't standing at the end of the alley, but his own sweat glands were pumping like Clint was standing in front of him with his right hand ready to draw.

A sound enters the alley, but it's not the jingle of spurs nor is it the crash of bodies diving into metal trash cans. A rustling sound comes from the wall of bushes to the left. Rob continues stepping forward, but moves closer to the wall of the building away from the bushes. The "first door you see" was at the end of the alley, still a good fifty feet away. Realizing he's being watched, Rob quickens his pace and puffs out his chest. Behind Rob the rustling in the bushes increases. As the sound grows louder Rob decides to confront his pursuer and quickly turns around to see...a cat.

Rob sighs, wipes some sweat from his brow, and turns back around to find two more cats immediately in front of him with another three further up the alley headed his way. A glance behind him reveals three more cats bounding towards him. If this was another movie surely an evil madman's minions were sent here to either carry off our hero or devour him right here in the alley. But the cats weren't hissing, meowing, or yowling. They were circling Rob, but they were not intimidating in their movements. In fact, the group, now at least a dozen strong, all had their tails straight up at attention and seemed to be herding Rob towards the lone metal, unmarked door on the side of the building. The movie scene that did enter Rob's thoughts was *Close Encounters of the Third Kind*. Rob was Richard Dreyfuss at the end of the film being encircled, welcomed, and guided toward the entrance of the alien craft by hoards of creepy, yet friendly, extraterrestrial beings.

"Sorry guys, I don't have anything for you," explained Rob as he reached for the doorknob.

"These ribs must be incredible," thought Rob as he entered the room. The back entrance to Mostly Franks was mostly a storage room. A concrete floor with cinder block walls, this room clearly wasn't part of the original building. Sometime in the last fifty years Frank must have needed a storage closet so he added on this ten-foot by ten-foot room off the back of the original building. The room was crowded: an ice machine, stacked flats of soda cans, towers of cardboard boxes labeled napkins, an old red hand cart, various other boxes of supplies, and three humans leaning against the cinder block walls. All illuminated by a single bare light bulb dropped down on a cord from the exposed wooden rafters above.

None of the humans were speaking, just standing in available spots between a push broom, a rolling yellow mop bucket, a wall mounted fire extinguisher, and another door that must have led inside Franks.

"Ribs?" asked Rob. Which was answered with an affirmative nod and a similar finger gesture that he got at the front door indicating his place to stand. Rob assumed his position between a push broom and an electrical panel box.

A few moments of awkward elevator ride silence was interrupted by the interior door opening. A small, middle-aged, hairy woman appeared holding a brown bag. She handed the bag to the man closest to her saying "Three pounds, twenty-seven dollars." As the door opened Rob caught a quick view of part of a kitchen and a few small card tables with red and white checked tablecloths. The transaction completed, the man exited, and the two other humans moved up one space. Being no dummy Rob took his cue and moved up to the spot next to the rolling yellow mop bucket.

Before Rob could finish investigating the contents of the mop bucket, the hairy woman had returned handing four bags to the guy next to the door saying, "Twenty pounds, one hundred eighty dollars."

"Must be a party," thought Rob as he prepared to move up to the fire extinguisher.

Several more minutes of elevator silence and the hairy woman appeared again, "One pound, nine dollars."

"Clearly a bachelor," Rob mused silently as he took a closer look at kitchen before the door closed. It looked clean and the card tables were full of people who appeared to be happily enjoying their meal. Rob stepped up to the number one position between the interior door and the fire extinguisher. With his cash in hand he felt this was more like a drug deal than picking up some ribs. But maybe these ribs were addictive.

Just then the exterior door opened with an innocent looking man in his thirties poking his head inside asking, "Ribs?"

Like an old pro Rob lifted a finger and silently pointed to the spot next to the rolling yellow mop bucket. The elevator silence was no longer awkward as Rob confidently waited for the return of the hairy woman. After a few moments the exterior door opened again with Rob ready to lift his finger, but the elderly gentleman casually nodded knowingly taking his place between the rolling yellow mop bucket and the push broom. Rob's disappointment at not getting to use his finger was short lived with the quick return of the hairy woman saying, "Ten pounds, ninety dollars." Rob slipped her the cash and received his two large, brown bags.

Feeling like a Columbian drug lord, Rob exited the room with his stash under his arms and was immediately confronted by the same gang of cats he had met earlier. The gang seemed tougher this time, crossing between Rob's legs and clawing at his pant legs. This appeared to be an organized feline attempt to take him down. But Rob was ready. He wasn't thinking of Redford as he walked back through the alley. Rob was Harrison Ford as Jack Ryan in *Clear and Present Danger*. Rob would make it safely out of this alley and back to the safety of his car no matter how many cats came after him. Nobody was going to take his stash away.

Turning the corner to the front side of Mostly Franks Rob found the gang of cats no long pursued him. Perhaps it was the buzz from the glowing neon sign, or the intimidating presence of the large man still guarding the front door, but Rob inwardly smiled and gave the behemoth at the door a proud nod. Rob knew he had outwitted, outmuscled, and defeated the gang on his own abilities. The ribs were safe.

With his adrenaline still pumping, an unexpected sound from the darkness "Rob?" caused our hero to jump, dropping both bags to the asphalt as the sound of his own name echoed across the parking lot.

"Rob, is that you?" repeated the voice.

"Yep, it's me," answered Rob shaking his head and surveying the damage to his goods.

"Sorry, I didn't mean to startle you, " responded the voice.

Rob looked up to see Danny Halton's smiling face and was quickly greeted with a warm embrace from an old friend. The two men dove into storytelling, catching up on what the other had been doing. After a few exchanges of the usual stories everyone has prepared for such unexpected encounters with old friends, Danny noticed that look on Rob's face. That same look from four years ago.

"Rob, it wasn't your fault. Laura and I had our problems. I made mistakes, so did she. What happened was our fault, not yours."

"But I've always felt if I hadn't shared that story..."

Danny cut him off, "If you hadn't shared that story it wouldn't have changed a thing. We just weren't right for each other. People grow and change. If Laura and I had stayed together we'd both be miserable right now. But today I'm happy and so is Laura."

"You talk to Laura?"

"Yes, I do Rob. She's married, living in Colorado, and has a kid. We've both moved on and it's time for you to move on too."

Danny's words were sincere and they did seem to help Rob feel better. "Is this what closure feels like?" thought Rob thinking about conversations he'd heard Jen share after she came home from book club. "No, I've got the perfect closure," he thought.

"You know what today is?" asked Rob grabbing Danny's arm. "USC vs. Notre Dame! I'm taking these ribs to Walt's place. You've got to come watch the game and try these ribs! They are supposed to be the best ribs in town."

"Thanks, but I've already got some plans tonight. You need to get yourself to Walt's before kickoff. Stay in touch, okay?"

"Thanks for talking Danny. I'm glad you're happy."

As Danny walked away and Rob entered his car Danny called back, "Hey Rob! You're right about those ribs. Best in town."

With the aroma of barbecue ribs filling the car, Rob decided to make one more stop on the way to Walt's house. Rob stopped by his own house, burst in the front door, and announced that book club was being held in conjunction with football over at Walt and Barb's place.

As Rob pulled away from the house with Barb, Rebecca, and Jen in the car he noticed Maxine standing on her front porch. Rob waved to Maxine saying, "Thanks for the tip on the ribs."

"Mostly Franks. Best ribs in town, " stated Maxine.

And Maxine was right.

Animal Control officials would like to remind drivers that due to a good rainy season and an abundance of food supply there has been a spike in the local skunk and deer population. This has led to a corresponding increase in the number of animal vs. vehicle accidents and service calls to remove animal carcasses.

While running over a skunk, dead or alive, is never a good idea running into a deer is much worse. Remember to avoid hitting our animal friends, but drastically swerving to miss them often leads to a worse outcome.

Drive carefully.

CHAPTER TWENTY

The Skunk & Deer Incident

Everyone around town has had a run in with a wild critter at some point, but John and Rebecca Forrester have had more than their share lately. With a name like Forrester you might assume the couple had a positive relationship with animals, but you would be wrong. Ever since the incident where the Forrester's dog Reni, short for Renaissance Mutt, had been electrocuted and nearly fried by his master, the animal kingdom seemed to have vengeance on its collective mind. Local wildlife no longer came after Reni, it was clear they were after John and Rebecca.

Living in the foothills means living with skunks. Living with skunks means not leaving dog food out on your porch or deck. Living with dog food in your house means living with the aroma of dog food in your house. And yes, living with dog food aroma in your house means living with skunks who want to get in your house.

None of this was news to anyone until John and Rebecca encountered a particularly persistent skunk. After several nights in a row of the distinctive sulfurous odor wafting through the house and keeping them awake, John realized the visitor must have decided to camp out in the crawl space beneath their house. In the morning John investigated all possible entry points for a skunk to access the crawl space and fortunately found one ventilation screen had come loose providing easy entry. John simply replaced the screen and the problem was solved. Of course, if the problem was solved this wouldn't be much of a skunk incident now would it?

Sure enough, that evening the pungent odor was back stinking up the house yet again, leading Rebecca to ponder, "Maybe you trapped him under the house when you fixed the screen." Sounds reasonable thought John.

"I'm on it!" proclaimed John hopping out of bed. Grabbing some tools from the garage, the pajama clad home protector went outside and removed the ventilation screen he had just repaired. Rebecca brought out a blanket and the two homeowners snuggled on a garden bench waiting to see if Rebecca's supposition was correct.

Snuggling under a blanket on a garden bench in the moonlight can lead to various outcomes, but in our incident the smooching was interrupted by a cute little inquisitive skunk venturing out into the world leaving the crawl space of the Forrester's home behind. Satisfied with their outfoxing the animal world, John replaced the screen and then he and Rebecca went back inside to continue their smooching and bask in their victory.

Until the next night.

"Maybe there was more than one skunk?" posed Rebecca holding her nose.

"Let's go!" replied John and the couple successfully repeated the same screen removal and snuggling process as last night.

A few minutes into this round of smooching, once again a skunk wandered out from beneath the house. "I think that is the same skunk," stated an irritated Rebecca.

"How can you tell?"

"Because he's staring at us. I recognize those eyes," answered Rebecca.

"I'm sure there aren't any other holes. I've checked everywhere," insisted John as he replaced the screen again.

"I'm going to follow him."

"Just keep your distance Rebecca. It's a skunk."

With an agitated Rebecca on point, the couple quietly followed the skunk along the side of the house and watched him turn the corner to the rear of the house. Reaching the corner John and Rebecca were surprised to see the skunk trot right up the steps to the back porch and disappear into the house.

"The dog door," spoke John with Rebecca in unison.

As John and Rebecca stood outside the kitchen door they realized they now had a much larger problem than a skunk living under the house. Entering the kitchen they saw what appeared to be a very relaxed skunk munching away at a bowl of dog kibble. Perhaps it was an instinctive move of a protective homeowner, or perhaps it was just stupid, but the first thing Rebecca did was start arguing with the skunk. "You can't be in here! Get out of my house!" were two of the yells discernible by John.

"Rebecca, it's a skunk. You're going to lose this argument," warned John.

Rebecca's second move was to grab a dishtowel in what appeared to be an attempt to herd the skunk. "Get the door open!" barked Rebecca.

John did as he was told, but also smiled as he noticed Rebecca's choice of a red towel made her look like a matador with the kitchen being the bull ring. But this bull was not about to charge the red cape. This skunk did what skunks always do. He lifted his tail, turned his body, and blasted his corrosive spray.

Rebecca turned to escape the acid cloud, fleeing to the bedroom locking the door behind her leaving John to fend for himself. Rebecca headed straight for the shower to begin the de-skunkification process while still wearing her pajamas. But not before giving an evil eye and "Where were you?" speech to Reni, who only seemed to acknowledge the situation by sneezing when Rebecca stormed past his bed.

John managed to step behind the kitchen door, successfully using it as a shield to deflect most of the blast. Still holding the door open John was hoping the skunk would declare victory and march out the door, but the skunk had other plans. He, or she, neither John or Rebecca could sex the skunk, strode over to the cabinets beneath the kitchen sink, dropped under the doors, and disappeared inside the cabinet.

"He's going after the kitchen trash. He's trapped in the cupboard," explained John to no one who was listening. Though his eyes were burning, John knew he couldn't pass up this chance to capture the skunk. With no Fish and Game Department skunk trap readily available, John grabbed the next best thing. A pot roast pan and lid that also doubled as the turkey pan at Thanksgiving. "If this thing has cooked a cow and cooked a bird, it can definitely cook a skunk," muttered John as he positioned himself on the floor.

Ready for battle, John flung open the cabinet doors only to find no skunk at all. Not in the trash bag, not in the recycling bag, not hiding behind the box of dishwashing detergent, there was no skunk in this cabinet. With John pondering the possibility of a molecular transporting device installed in his kitchen cabinetry, he became aware of a slight cool breeze on his feet. That was the moment John solved two mysteries: first, how the skunk was entering the crawl space; and second, why Rebecca commented on having cold feet when she was working at the kitchen sink.

The clever skunk had never entered the cabinet. When he dropped beneath the doors he disappeared through the air duct beneath the cabinets. The flexible heating and cooling duct tubing had disconnected from the vent beneath the cabinet. The skunk ducked right through the open vent, dropping into the crawl space below. Rebecca's cold toes where from cool air flowing up from beneath the house.

Wondering how long this neighborhood skunk had been working this gig of full kitchen access and free dog food, John locked the dog door, went outside and once again removed the outside screen to let the skunk out. The skunk was waiting for John to let him out as he left the crawl space before John had a chance to sit down on the bench. John replaced the screen and watched the skunk walk around the corner to the back of the house.

"Not anymore pal," boasted John watching a disappointed skunk push his head against a locked dog door.

Ready for a shower himself, John found himself locked out of his bedroom. He could hear the shower water still running and feel the steam rising from beneath the bedroom door, though he wondered if the steam was from the hot water or Rebecca's mood. Rebecca had obviously received the worst of the skunk's spray. Walking back to the kitchen John's first thought was perhaps it would just be easier to move and start over rather than to clean up a skunkified kitchen. But then he figured he'd have to clean the house before they sold it anyway, so he might as well get started.

Apples, bananas, a single grapefruit, a box of crackers, and a half-eaten bar of dark chocolate immediately went into the trash. As did everything else that was out on the counters. During the first few days John and Rebecca tossed about half of the food in the kitchen. Canned goods were safe, but it's difficult to enjoy minestrone soup when you're reminded of eau de skunk as you open the can. So most of the cans were tossed as well. At first

John thought he could save his beloved four-slice toaster, Rebecca's rather expensive automatic drip coffee maker, and the bread machine they'd been given for Christmas a few years back, but after a week of unsuccessful attempts with various cleaning solvents they too were dumped.

John was thankful the kitchen cabinetry was all painted wood. The oily skunk spray beaded on the gloss finish rather than penetrate the surface, so quick action of wiping the cabinets with a concoction of baking soda, hydrogen peroxide, and dishwashing liquid saved weeks of stinky wood. The Forresters had used the same mixture several times on Reni with success and John was appreciative of how well it worked on floors and counters too.

Before you start thinking, "What about tomato juice?" you should know you've just identified yourself as a flat lander or city slicker who watches a lot of television. Anyone with a dog who lives in the hills knows tomato juice doesn't do a darned thing to the oils in skunk spray. Tomato juice just masks the sulfur odor for a while making you smell like a ketchup factory. And if you don't clean up all the sweet tomato juice, the next problem you'll have is an invasion of ants.

Eventually a wet Rebecca entered the kitchen joining in the recovery process. All affected clothing, towels, and kitchen floor rugs went into the washing machine loaded up with bleach and set on the same "sanitary" cycle first time parents use when they insist on using cloth diapers and trying to clean them themselves. After the third run through the washer, Rebecca declared everything acceptable except her extra long, cotton sleeping shirt with the picture of the little girl from *Les Miserables* on the front.

Well past midnight John headed to the shower to begin his deskunkification process. But not before giving an evil eye and "Where were you?" speech to Reni, who only seemed to acknowledge the situation by sneezing when John stormed past his bed.

Six hours later John headed off to work and set up his classroom for the day. After his first encounter with the office staff, the secretaries said in unison, "You didn't get it all off," before John even had a chance to tell his story. Apparently some of the events of last night were obvious. "We'll call you a substitute for the day."

"Really?" asked John. "I can't smell anything. I thought I got it all."

"Go home!" was the command of the office ladies.

"But it's Open House tonight. I've got things to do."

"Go home. Now! Get yourself cleaned up and come back after school. Open House doesn't start until seven."

Knowing you don't mess with secretaries, John headed home for a few more rounds of bathing and scrubbing with baking soda, hydrogen peroxide, and dishwashing liquid. Rebecca's car in the driveway was a surprise until John found Rebecca soaking in the tub in a mixture of baking soda, hydrogen peroxide, and dishwashing liquid. Evidently secretaries in the real estate world had the same olfactory abilities and had commanded that their boss go home as well.

A little before five, a refreshed and clean smelling John Forrester headed back out on his thirty minute commute to work to prepare his classroom for the onslaught of thirty students and their parents who would soon descend upon his room. About a mile shy of school another member of the animal kingdom decided to inflict some havoc in John's life as a large deer barreled out of the trees and hit John's car in the right front corner. If you're thinking John hit the deer, you've once again identified yourself as a big city person. For insurance purposes, the car never hits the deer, the deer hits the car.

John was traveling forty miles an hour when the deer hit him, but when he pulled over to the side of the road there was no deer to be found. The headlamp and cover were broken, part of the front panel above the right front tire was smashed, but not infringing on the tire, and the front bumper and decorative grill were definitely going to need to be replaced. John wasn't hurt, just dazed and surprised not to see a dead buck in the road. Thinking perhaps killing a deer was his payback to Mother Nature for sending a skunk into his kitchen, John climbed back into his minivan and finished the short drive to work.

Not twenty minutes after walking into his classroom and setting up for the night's festivities, fellow teacher Barry Reese stuck his head in John's doorway with a huge smile on his face.

"John, come see what I've got in the back of my Subaru."

"Barry, you know I was out today. I've got work to do."

"No, really, you've got to see this," explained Barry as he walked into the room wearing a button down collar blue shirt covered with blood.

"Barry, are you okay? What happened?"

"I'm fine. Come on, you've got to see what I've got in the back of the car."

Ignoring the blood all over Barry's shirt and slacks was easy for Barry, but John needed more convincing his friend was uninjured before following Barry out to the parking lot.

Barry opened up the back hatch of his Subaru to reveal a dead buck sprawled out across the back of the vehicle. "He was on the side of the road, less than a mile from here," explained a giddy Barry.

John was stunned. Stunned on many levels. Certainly this was the deer he had just hit less than an hour ago, but if there was any question that doubt was removed by the pieces of clear plastic headlamp cover sticking out of the deer's side that looked eerily familiar to the missing headlamp cover pieces from John's minivan that was parked right next to Barry's Subaru. But mostly John was stunned because the two of them were standing in an elementary school parking lot looking at a bloody mess of a dead deer in the back of Barry's car.

Barry Reese, the Environmental Education Food Safety Activist, wasn't some hunter smiling about his out of season good fortune. Barry wasn't going to eat this. Barry rarely ate meat at all and when he did the meat had to be organic range fed cattle that had led a glorious, wonderful life listening to the wind blow through green grass while cavorting with all those happy cows that made the happy California cheese.

"Barry, what are you going to do with this?"

"For my class, my students. Native American lessons. We'll tan the hides. We'll use the brain enzymes to soften the hide. We'll make deer hoof rattles."

"'What do you mean *we*?" interrupted John.

Barry didn't stop, "We'll set the hooves on an ant hill and let the ants clean out all the meat. We'll use part of the hide to make a drum. We can use the sinew to attach pouches of sand to the leg bones for rhythm makers. The antlers are perfect for..."

Barry's monologue about the potential uses for a dead deer was paused by a twitching in the back of the Subaru. This wasn't one of those after death, nerve reaction death twitches. This twitch became a movement of a deer trying to kick his legs. This buck was trying to stand up in the back of the car. As the deer was rolling around blood began to gush out the deer's mouth, nose, and heavily injured side.

"Barry, you forgot to check to see if this guy was dead," was more of a statement than question.

Not knowing what to do with a bloody buck thrashing around in the back of a car, information not currently found in the owner's manuals of most vehicles, Barry slammed closed the hatch saying, "What the hell do we do now?"

"Why do you keep saying *we*? This is *your* car and *your* deer."

"Well, we've got to do something. Students and parents are going to start rolling in here in an hour."

"Again, what's with the *we*?" expressed John as the Subaru was now rocking and moist blood smears were visible all over the rear windows.

"We can't let him out here. It'll be a mess and kids will watch this guy die. He won't make it. We've got to put him out of his misery. What can we use? What have you got in your car?"

Not surprisingly John Forrester doesn't carry a spear, bow, or even a buck knife in his minivan. John had what he usually had sitting around the back of all of his vehicles.

"You owe me for this one," said John looking at the array of weapons. John selected a jagged piece of quartz he'd found a few weeks ago on a hike around an old gold mine. Barry chose a grapefruit sized river rock that had caught Rebecca's eye on a picnic along the American River just last weekend. Neither of these rocks would ever reach their original destination as part of the Forrester's landscaping plans. These two murderous rocks would have a different destiny eventually being washed off near the bus garage and casually discarded behind the garage in the school storage lot appropriately nicknamed *The Boneyard*.

With the now permanently quieted buck laying still beneath some newspapers and a small tarp meant to hold rocks, the carcass carrying Subaru was moved to a more discrete location and the minivan was shuffled over to cover a few incriminating stains on the asphalt.

After the deed, the two blood splattered men, public employees, educators of young minds, guardians of the future looked at each other with the same thought: "You can't run an Open House looking like you're a psychopathic murderer fresh from his latest kill."

Rummaging through the lost and found bin in the gymnasium revealed only two possibilities for replacing blood splattered clothing: a large, youth-sized, pink t-shirt with "Barbie" written in glittery cursive across the front, and a fur-lined winter coat. Both of which must have belonged to large sixth-grade girls and may have raised more questions with the community than the blood stained shirts and ties they were currently wearing. With time running out John thought of one other idea.

And so, Mr. Reese spent the evening of Open House wearing a white science lab coat, proclaiming the value of science in education, while Mr. Forrester extolled the virtues of working hard, earning a high school diploma, and going to college while sporting a blue graduation gown, mortarboard cap, and yellow tassel.

If anyone noticed the missing costumes from the drama closet, they never said a word. If any parent noticed that Mr. Reese and Mr. Forrester were wearing only boxers and briefs respectively beneath their attire, they never said a word. If any student noticed their teachers were wearing wet, recently rinsed shoes with no socks, they never said a word. If any custodian noticed the bloody clothing in the bottom of Mr. Forrester's trash can...they never said a word.

When the evening was finished and the costumed deer slayers were walking out to their vehicles, the men stopped at John's minivan. John reflected on the events of the last twenty-four hours, "Barry, I don't want to know what you're going to do with the buck. I think I've done my part. I'm going home and spend some time with Reni. Obviously, Mother Nature feels I haven't truly apologized for electrocuting my dog."

Barry thanked and hugged his friend in the graduation gown, realizing their friendship had reached yet another level in male relationship bonding. As John backed out of the parking space, Barry shared one final thought, "Hey John, what did you do to the front of your van?"

Locals know when putting snow chains on your tires in inclement weather it is a good idea to pull over to the side of the road as far as possible. If the plow approaches while you're working, your best bet to avoid the oncoming wave of flying snow and slush produced by the four-foot tall, eight-foot wide blade is to crouch down low behind your vehicle or wait inside until the plow passes safely by.

Newcomers Tino and Lisa De Luca would also like to add it is a good idea to make sure your vehicle's windows and doors are closed as well. No permanent damage was done to their four-door sedan by the surge of flying snow that swamped the inside of their vehicle, but the young couple did find they had a very wet ride home from the grocery store.

CHAPTER TWENTY-ONE

The De Luca Reunion

Most folks enjoy the De Luca family as soon as they meet them. Tino and Lisa De Luca are a pair of friendly thirty-year-olds with two young kids who cashed out of life in the big city to lead a more relaxed life in the foothills. Leaving behind two promising careers in the computer industry was tough, but selling their modest Bay Area home at the height of the market produced a windfall that would stretch much further in the foothills than it would in the city.

Real Estate agent Rebecca Forrester first liked the De Lucas because they were a young family looking for a house with a little property. After learning about their large Italian family, which meant the possibility of more clients, Rebecca liked them even more. Eventually Rebecca came to treasure the De Luca family for their warmth, kindness, and generosity...which was handy since she sold them a three-bedroom, two-bath house on two slightly sloped acres just down the road from her own home.

Rebecca's husband, landscape enthusiast John, enjoyed becoming casual friends with Tino and Lisa, but the friendship was truly cemented when Tino offered to take care of the Forrester's yard while John and Rebecca went out of town for a week. John instructed Tino with all the usuals: feed the cats, water the potted plants, pick up the newspaper and mail, and give the fish in the koi pond a few pinches of fish food a couple of times a day. Taking care of the koi pond is what showed John what a good friend Tino would become.

Tino and Lisa had been in the Forrester's backyard paradise many times and the two were actually looking forward to spending a little time alone with their kids taking advantage of everything the yard offered. A little tag with the boys on the grass followed by an introductory lesson to bocce on the decomposed granite playing surface. Some wandering on the pathways, rock climbing on the retaining walls, and of course John and Rebecca had encouraged the De Lucas to harvest anything that was ripe. Strawberries, blueberries, cherries, peaches, tomatoes, and peppers were all ready for picking. Sitting on the stones around the pond and munching on strawberries with his boys, Tino became concerned by the water level in the koi pond. The level was much lower than it had been several days ago and Tino was concerned for the safety of the fish.

Knowing there was a specialized filter in the pond, not knowing the water quality requirements for koi, and certainly not wanting to lose any exotic fish on his watch, Tino decided to raise the level of the pond by adding filtered water. But the only source of filtered water he knew of was the refrigerator back in his own kitchen. So it was that Tino, Lisa, and the boys spent the better part of a Saturday afternoon filling up three ice chests in their kitchen using the filtered drinking water from their refrigerator tap, loading up the ice chests in the back of their pickup, driving up to the Forrester's place, lugging the chests to the backyard, and dumping the filtered drinking water in the pond. Tino knew koi were an expensive investment and he did not want the Forresters coming home to a sad and depleted pond. Tino later explained they must have made at least four trips to bring the water level up to what he thought was an acceptable height.

When John heard of the De Luca's efforts on behalf of his fish, he almost didn't have the heart to tell Tino and Lisa that of the dozen fish in the pond only two were genuine koi purchased for a buck and half each. The remaining ten "koi" were feeder fish. The little guys you buy at ten for a dollar and feed to turtles, frogs, and bigger fish. John and Rebecca had given up on expensive koi and gone with plain old goldfish several years ago after the local raccoon population had discovered their backyard and turned the pond into their favorite sushi hangout. As for the filtered water, John appreciated their efforts, but he knew he had to show Tino the hose curled up behind the waterfall for future house sitting occasions.

Lovable klutz Walt Peterson liked the De Luca family before he even met them. When Walt heard the story about Tino filling the pond with filtered water, he heard the long version. The version where Tino was on his fourth round of filling the ice chests in his kitchen, getting a little tired, and knocking out the plug in the bottom of the chest leaking cool filtered water all over his tile floor. Which led to Tino picking up the chest, slipping on the water, and knocking his head against the edge of the kitchen counter. The resulting cut didn't require stitches, just a butterfly bandage. Regardless, when Walt heard this chain of events he felt an instant bond with the man.

Even forgetful Barry Reese felt close to the De Luca family after a recent roadside incident on a snowy day. Apparently Tino and Lisa were not familiar with the procedure of putting tire chains on their family sedan. As they sat in the car reading directions on how to chain up, the windows began to fog so Tino rolled down the window to get some fresh air. Once the couple felt confident they got out of the car to begin their task. As they heard the large snow plow approaching with it's monstrous blade scraping the pavement throwing a wall of snow, slush, and ice off to the side of the road, the couple wisely retreated behind their vehicle shielding themselves from the blast. Only after the plow passed did Tino and Lisa realize the importance of closing the door and rolling up the window before the plow arrives. The two boys in the backseat were just fine and actually thought the wave of snow entering the car was fun with six-year-old Michael yelling, "Do it again Dad!" No permanent damage was done to their sedan, but Tino and Lisa had a very wet ride home from the grocery store.

The De Luca family offered something for everyone. Rob and Jennifer Taylor liked them for security purposes. With a guy named Rocco De Luca living in the neighborhood surely crime rates in the area would stay low or perhaps be nonexistent. Who would want to mess with a guy named Rocco De Luca, and when you add in his brother Michael, *forgetaboutit*. Of course if they knew Rocco De Luca was a four-year-old who spends most of his day running around the yard in his Spider-man underwear they might feel differently.

Octogenarian Mary Thorpe was taken with the family after chancing upon them in the pet food aisle. A polite conversation about cats stopped her failing eyesight from buying six cans of Little Friskies' turkey giblets rather than Carrot's preferred ocean whitefish.

Only fellow octogenarian Maxine Baxter didn't take an immediate liking to the new family in town. Some thought perhaps her feelings were due to childhood memories of Italians and the War. Others thought perhaps she was just getting old and did not want any newcomers in her life. Only Maxine's husband Clarence understood the real reason for her dislike of Italians had more to do with his own fascination and preoccupation with Sophia Loren during the 1960's. Clarence was always a Sophia Loren fan, but after seeing her in *Marriage-Italian Style* on a Friday night in 1964, there was an unfortunate incident involving Clarence speaking to Sophia in his sleep. Maxine was awakened by the pillow talk between her husband and the Italian bombshell and did not appreciate the topics discussed in their conversation. Clarence's mooning over Sophia was over long ago, but since that time Clarence knew two items to be true. He no longer watched Italian movies and any Italians in town had to earn the respect and friendship of his wife.

After eight months of the De Lucas living in town, the community's love and acceptance of the Italian family was put to the test at the end of their first summer as residents. The De Lucas were set to have their annual family reunion at Tino and Lisa's new home. Tino was the youngest of seven, so just his immediate family of siblings and spouses, along with Mama and Pop De Luca would be a crowd. Add in everyone's children, and some of those children are now adults themselves, throw in a few boyfriends and girlfriends and you're up over fifty people. Mix in some cousins with their broods along with all the families in the neighborhood and you're at seventy-five easy. Toss in a few new acquaintances from around town along with a few random Italians and you're not too far from one hundred guests attending the De Luca family reunion.

Brothers and sisters starting showing up late Thursday afternoon. Oldest brother Tony arrived first so he and Tino could begin setting up the portable five-hole miniature golf course he'd brought up from San Jose. Tony borrowed the course from a preschool his neighbor owned. The school used the course at fundraisers throughout the year and Tony thought this would be something new for all the kids to do during the weekend. They needed a lot of the flat driveway space and wanted to claim the area before other vehicles crowded in.

Assembling the course took most of the evening because the workers were continually interrupted by the arrival of more De Lucas. Though the pace of assembly picked up as more hands joined the team, the volume of opinions picked up as well. Quality control was maintained by Lisa who did a skillful job of distributing beer based on body weight and motor control.

Numerous children spent the evening running around and through the construction zone hoping to be the first on the course. The only casualty occurred when Tino and Lisa's six-year-old Michael whacked a yellow golfball through the open drawbridge on the front of the castle. A beautiful shot whose only problem was four-year-old Rocco sitting inside the castle opening his mouth in sequence with the drawbridge.

Because arrival times were so scattered the food plan for the evening was just pizza. Three pizzas were delivered at five o'clock, three more at seven, and another round at nine. Pizza seems anticlimactic for a large group of Italians, but everyone knew there would be no shortage of food this weekend. With full bellies, tired bodies, and one ice pack on Rocco's lower lip, all Italians were quiet on the De Luca property by midnight.

By late Friday afternoon the Italian population in town had doubled. Some stayed at nearby motels, but most spread out around the De Luca's house claiming sleeping locations on all available beds, couches, recliners, and open floor space. Four tents were set up outside for the younger crowd while a camper in the bed of a pickup and a small Winnebago were parked off the driveway in one of the open grassy areas on the De Luca's two-acre property.

Propane and charcoal grills were fired up cooking a selection of barbecue ribs and chicken, along with the always popular burgers and dogs. Horseshoes, bocce, Frisbee golf, and mini golf were in action by all ages. A pair of card tables were set up, one for scopa and the other for briscola. The older crowd hoping to pass down their beloved card games to the younger generation, even if the kids only saw the games once a year. The ice chests, filled with water, soda, and juices, were everywhere. For the wine, beer, limoncello, and any other hard stuff you had to go up on the deck on the front of the house. That was Lisa's rule, she would tolerate no stumbling or slurring Italians around all these kids. And like all good Italian mothers, her rules were obeyed.

The host also gets to choose the movies shown during the weekend. The only rule was the movie had to have an Italian as a main character. Friday night had lots of the ladies inside the house swooning over *Moonstruck*, while Tino set up *Jaws* to be shown outside. When questioned about who was the Italian in *Jaws*, Tino explained, "Anytime that shark eats he has some sauce dribbling out of his mouth, so he has to be one of us." Tino's logic was accepted and Spielberg's classic was projected on the front of the garage door. Which worked well except the five times during the film when non-movie watchers exited the house through the garage and hit the automatic garage door opener causing the retreat of the movie screen.

Midway through Friday night John and Rebecca Forrester came down for a visit and were warmly greeted as honorary Italians. Noting the size of the crowd, John realized the De Luca's had never had one of these family gatherings outside the realm of a city sewer system. John pulled Tino aside and explained to his neighbor about the limits of a septic tank system built for a three-bedroom, two-bathroom house, leading Tino to arrange an emergency nighttime delivery of two very nice port-a-pots. Nice ones, big enough to stand up and stretch in, even do a little tap dance if that's your thing. Bright blue fiberglass boxes with hand washing stations and mirrors on the inside. Port-a-pots that were quickly dressed up on the outside with pictures from *Star Wars* and *Spider-man* wall calendars not quite happily donated by Michael and Rocco De Luca. Between these two stations, two bathrooms in the house, one in the camper, one in the RV, and the close proximity of a thick wall of oleander bushes on the north side of the property, and an equally thick wall of blackberry bushes on the south, any potential septic disasters were averted.

Anyone living on the north side of town had a good idea of what time it was by listening to the style of music emanating from the De Luca reunion. If you stuck your head outside your home and heard Bruce Springsteen, Madonna, or Lady Gaga you knew it was late afternoon. If you heard Frank Sinatra, Tony Bennett, or Bobby Darin you figured it must be time to eat. When Jim Croce started playing you knew it was close to bed time. But when the heavy metal strands of Metallica rattled the windows in your home, you rolled over and looked at the clock, aggravated to see it was after midnight. Sound carries well through the hills so Tino wasn't surprised to see the local cops roll in and tell him to turn it down, way down, "so folks on the other side of town can sleep."

The officers stayed awhile checking out the De Luca crowd, but left after fifteen minutes, convinced the De Lucas were under control. Interestingly enough, Officer Bercelli returned Saturday night as well, though not in uniform. Carlo Bercelli and his fiance Anna brought three bottles of chianti and a half-dozen loaves of garlic bread. The chianti did nothing to help Carlo's skill at bocce, but it did make him a talkative partner for Pop De Luca as they discussed in Italian the best strategy for blocking their opponents approach to the pallino.

Most of Saturday's activities centered around food. Semolina flour was used to form several different pastas: spaghetti, of course, but also linguine, fettuccine, and enough lasagna for a few deep dish pans. Pasta was mixed, kneaded, rolled, pressed, cranked, and extruded all morning long.

The main event was making the ravioli. Once the pasta was rolled out into four-inch wide, twelve-inch long sheets, each bottom strip was sent outside to one of several filling stations. All of this work has to be done quickly so the pasta doesn't dry out. Spoons and melon ball scoopers were used to drop the filling on the lower sheet which was then covered with a top sheet. Squeezing out the air and sealing each ravioli is important so the trapped air doesn't expand and cause your ravioli to explode during cooking.

Mama De Luca was spooning out Tino's favorite filling, ground italian sausage with spinach, oregano, sage, and lots of ricotta cheese. Lisa was using a new recipe this year with portobello mushrooms, olive oil, Italian parsley, ricotta cheese, and some garlic. Rebecca Forrester came down to help Tony's wife Carolyn with her crab filling with lemon, onions, garlic, capers, black pepper, a little fennel, and a lot of butter, which would be served with a creamy, white-wine sauce. Tino's sister Joanie and her husband Danny were working with several concoctions: one with goat cheese, another with lamb and tarragon, and a third more traditional recipe using ground beef blended with a marinara sauce.

Once appropriately filled, covered, and squeezed, each ravioli was cut using pastry wheels, ravioli cutters, knives, and cookie cutters making sure each ravioli had its own unique shape to go with its own unique taste. Each chef had a team with at least three pairs of small extra hands to keep the pasta moving from the kitchen to filling stations and to the refrigerators and ice chests all the while keeping the precious pasta moist.

While the De Lucas were anxiously awaiting the evening meal to dine on all of these wonderful creations, a pair of late entries to the table were undoubtably the most appreciated. Though Maxine Baxter was invited to the De Luca reunion, there was no way she would ever agree to be surrounded by so many Italians. But after Jennifer Taylor stopped by Saturday morning and shared with Maxine some of the details of what a wonderful family gathering this event was, Maxine's respect for love of family overcame her dislike of Sophia Loren. When Maxine realized just how many family members were attending this reunion, she felt the need to honor that commitment to family. Of course that's what the De Luca's heard, even if the actual comment to Rebecca was, "There's nothing worse than a bunch of hungry Italians in the neighborhood." But somewhere deep inside Maxine felt the need to be hospitable as she harvested nearly her entire crop of basil from her garden and made the largest batch of her homemade pesto she could ever recall. She also pulled out five quarts of her homemade tomato sauce she'd put up earlier in the summer. As she brought everything over to Jennifer Saturday afternoon in an oversized wicker basket with fresh-cut roses laying atop the jars she grumbled, "Tell those hooligans to keep it down tonight."

With the evening's prep work all done, the Italian hooligans were now ready to take a family walk and build up an appetite for Saturday night's final meal together. Though no known city ordinance prevents large groups of Italians from walking down Main Street, the De Lucas did realize the sight of fifty or sixty Italians filling the downtown sidewalks in a single mob might be a bit intimidating for the average shopper. So the De Lucas broke up into smaller groups, some by marriage or impending marriage, some by common interests or assumed common interests, and some by who had the best ability with the younger kids to both keep them out of the street and keep them from annoying the community as a whole with their repeated requests to enter the three candy stores downtown has to offer.

Some of the latter group, which included several teenagers, were particularly fascinated with the structure of the Bell Tower located smack in the middle of Main Street. Constructed of thin metal pieces looking like an miniature Eiffel Tower on a severe no-carb diet, the Bell Tower presented the teens with the obvious question of "Can we climb to the top?" The expected answer didn't stop the conversations, challenges, and bets as to who could be the fastest to climb to the top and ring the bell.

Meanwhile across the street a dozen Italians paused in front of the wine tasting bar until a voice from six shops further down bellowed, "Don't even think about it!" Mama De Luca's command was obeyed and the group moved on down to the music store to browse without Mama's presence.

Proclaiming all Italians are loud is certainly overstating a cultural bias, but stating the De Luca family is loud is certainly being kind. The volume level is always high and to many folks the voices sound like arguing. But to those in the De Luca family if you didn't speak loudly you weren't heard. If you weren't heard you didn't have an opinion. Volume and opinion went hand in hand, and opinions were often diverse which meant you had to be louder than the other opinion. Outsiders were often shocked at the combination of volume, emotion, and facial expression that went into conversation, but once you got to know the De Lucas you knew they weren't mad at you or anyone else, they were just expressing their opinions.

Since not everyone in the general public walking downtown Saturday afternoon knew this conversational attribute about the De Lucas, they tended to give each of the Main Street De Luca groups a wide berth when the Italians approached. Unsuspecting tourists and locals could be seen ducking into shops they had absolutely no interest in visiting. Ladies found themselves momentarily looking at baseball memorabilia in Empire Sports Cards while some men tried to look casual standing next to a selection of ladies undergarments at Marlene's, For the Mature Woman.

Upon hearing four loud dongs from the Bell Tower, all the De Luca groups left Main Street eliciting an almost audible sigh from the local shops that seemed to calm all of downtown. Even the Bell Tower appeared as if it had less to worry about. Amoebae-like blobs of Italians funneled down to ants marching two by two along the sidewalks until the concrete walkways yielded to dirt pathways ultimately reaching Tino and Lisa's property.

Early Saturday evening the grills that had been so busily barbecuing yesterday were immediately put to use boiling water. Lots of pasta varieties meant lots of boiling pots of water. Sauces and toppings were warmed on every available grill, griddle, hot plate, and camp stove. Breads, prepared and plain, were placed in serving trays warmed from below by canned flames and candles. Chianti was flowing, having replaced most of the beer, and children were pumped with caffeinated beverages.

Paper plates and plastic utensils had been replaced with compostable plates and soy-based utensils thanks to a generous contribution from the local Environmental Education Food Safety Activist Barry Reese. When Mama De Luca asked, "Who is Barry?" and "What is an EEFSA?" she understood the abridged answer of "He's the guy to wants to save the whales." Mama and Pop wanted to meet Barry but he had been a no show all weekend. He'd been invited to the reunion, but rumor was he had a hot date this weekend. Of course the chances were just as good that the absent-minded Barry forgot about the De Luca gathering.

The cooking never really stopped and the formal eating never really began. One just melded with the other. There were no lines or crowds at the serving tables just a constant flow of Italians like waves washing up on the shore. The miniature golf course would be momentarily void of participants only to be filled again by golfers attempting to putt with a mouth full of lasagna and a club covered with garlic butter. Bocce became a sport now dependent on two skills, your proximity to the pallino and your ability to balance a glass of chianti.

Walt and Barb Peterson arrived just at the moment a propane tank on one of the grills needed to be replaced. Wanting to help Walt offered to switch out the tanks, but somehow all the De Lucas had been advised not to accept Walt's kind offers of assistance. A compromise was reached when Walt was draped with a red apron and put in charge of serving marinara sauce. Barb was enjoying her ravioli with portobello mushrooms and the lessons on scopa she was receiving from Mama De Luca.

Smiling, laughing, happy people were everywhere. Tino and Lisa couldn't be more pleased. "Funiculi, Funicula" was playing and the earth beneath their feet seemed to carry the beat and fill their souls with joy. Everything that was dear to them was within their vision. Michael and Rocco playing in the dirt with cousins. Brothers and sisters telling stories about the old days and dreams of what was yet to come. Mama and Pop happily passing along their traditions to family, new friends, and friends to be. Neighbors and friends who had so warmly welcomed them to this place and this town.

"Bella familia," said Tino.

Looking into her husband's eyes Lisa agreed, "Bella familia."

As evening turned to darkness, many De Lucas began the long process of saying goodbye, offering their thanks, hugs, and well-wishes before hitting the road for their journeys home. A campfire was burning near the vegetable garden with a farewell dessert, a roasted marshmallow with a warm chocolate peanut butter cup sandwiched between two graham crackers, made by each family as they left. The dessert was a reminder that the time the De Luca family spent together was a cherished sweetness, and goodbyes were nothing to be sad about.

John and Rebecca Forrester walked back up the hill to their home turning around to see the happy Italian faces warmed by the fire.

"Beautiful family," said John.

"Beautiful family," smiled Rebecca.

By Sunday afternoon the town's population returned to normal. Though with the amount of food, alcohol, and music available over the last three days odds are pretty good the Italian population will increase by at least a few for next year's De Luca family reunion.

Department of Fish and Game officials responded to a call of a bear in a tree yesterday. The bear was too high in the tree to use a tranquilizer gun. Officers said the bear wouldn't survive the fall, so they put out a bear trap at the base of the tree. The trap was baited with a tuna fish sandwich and some peanut butter spread on apple slices. Officers said to just give the bear some time and he'll come down.

Rebecca Forrester stated she wasn't too sure about peanut butter, perhaps they should try chocolate frosting. We'll keep you posted.

CHAPTER TWENTY-TWO

Rebecca's Bear

Bears are not common around here, but you can't say they are rare. Once or twice a year someone around town has an encounter, usually due to an uncovered trash can or some unattended food sitting outside. But yesterday's adventure at the Forrester's home gave additional weight to the theory of the continuing efforts on the part of the animal kingdom to extract some revenge on John and Rebecca Forrester for electrocuting and nearly killing their dog Reni.

Wednesday morning Rebecca planned to leave the house about seven and go to work at her real estate office like any other Wednesday morning. But when Rebecca opened the front door she found herself face to face with a rather large, imposing black bear who appeared ready to knock on the door or at least ring the doorbell. Rebecca yelled, screamed might be more accurate, turned, and ran back inside the house. Yes, you guessed it. Without closing the front door.

In her panic to escape the bear and retreat behind the door of her master bedroom, which she did remember to close, she had unknowingly laid out the red carpet for the bear to enter the house and head straight for the kitchen. Hearing the grunts and banging taking place in her kitchen on just the other side of a now rather wimpy, thin feeling, bedroom door, Rebecca decided to further her retreat and head outside through the bedroom sliding glass door. On her way out she caught a glance of Reni, her lovable Renaissance Mutt, laying comfortably on his dog bed and yelled, "What happened to our Bear Dog?"

The words spoken to Reni were meant to be encouragement, reminding Reni of his heroic actions in what happened on a similar morning just two years ago.

Anyone who lives in the foothills and has a dog knows when the dog is in the house and starts barking like a crazed beast, jumping at the windows, and causing general destruction inside, the last thing you do is let your dog outside. He has probably seen or smelled a deer and if you let him outside you might not see your dog until the end of the day, if you're lucky. So when Reni was jumping like a pogo stick and barking at the front door at six in the morning, no way was John going to let him out. As Reni's antics progressed to the family room and he began frantically scratching and whining at the glass door, Rebecca said, "No chance Reni. I'm not letting you chase some deer all over town." But when Reni reached the ten-minute mark of jumping, barking, howling, and thoroughly making a pest of himself at the kitchen door, John relented and let Reni out on to the back deck. Reni flew out the door and made an immediate right turn with his feet losing their grip on the wood planks. Scrambling his rear legs for traction, Reni's claws found a grip and the agitated dog flashed down the stairs, with a now curious John and Rebecca following close behind.

At the top of the stairs the Forresters saw what Reni had smelled, a large black bear was in the backyard calming walking across the bocce court. Calmly walking until he saw Reni charging at him. With no fear, Reni bolted at full speed straight toward the bear. Calling on her border collie instincts, Reni barked, chased, and herded the bear across the yard into the fruit orchard. The size of the bear made his speed deceptive. Though he appeared to be lumbering at a casual pace across the yard, John and Rebecca's viewpoint allowed them to see the amount of ground the bear covered with each step. The bear was moving at a fast clip equal to Reni's sheepherding speed.

Reni cornered the bear between a pair of apricot trees and a six-foot tall, no climb fence. Apparently bears don't know about "no climb" fencing material because when this bear stood up on his hind legs, with his head looking over the top of the fence, he scrambled right up to the top where his sizable weight made the metal fence sag in a two-foot dip. The bear dropped to the ground on the other side with a thud the Forresters felt all the way up on the deck. The invading bear ran away and never looked back. Reni continued jumping, barking, and running along the fence line seemingly challenging the beast to come back and try to trespass on his family's domain again. With no thought for his safety or realization the mighty bear could have destroyed him with a single swipe, Reni had saved his family.

Since that day Reni patrolled the property with his head held higher and his gait grown stronger. Reni was now a "Bear Dog," master of the property, guardian of the family, and protector of all that is sacred to dog and man. A dog with attitude. Out of respect for their Bear Dog's accomplishment, John and Rebecca left the sag in the fence as evidence of Reni's bear chasing and home protection valiance. Visitors to the property were taken to the historical site, shown the evidence, and told the tale of Reni's great deed.

But what about now? Here was another bear and this one was *inside* the house. Here was another chance for Reni the Bear Dog to leap into action and prove his valor. But the guardian of the family was currently more interested in repositioning his head away from the noise coming from the other room.

As Rebecca stood outside in the morning sunshine, listening to the carnage taking place in her kitchen, looking at Reni curled up on his bed, and remembering his former bravery, she found courage in herself. Mixed in with the courage was a growing sense of anger. Anger that a bear was currently enjoying free rein in her house.

If you're a Hobbit, courage and anger can combine to help you destroy all the evil forces of Middle-earth. If you're real estate agent Rebecca Forrester, courage and anger can combine to help you make some questionable decisions.

Remembering that she had already lost a battle with a skunk, Rebecca vowed not to be defeated again by the forces of the animal kingdom. Rebecca Forrester decided to take back her house from the marauding bear. Charging back into the bedroom, she looked for weapons. Finding none, she turned to Reni for advice who responded with an unusual and audible high pitched yawn.

"That's it! Noise! We need to make lots of noise!" Rebecca agreed.

That was always the advice to ward off bears. Look big and make lots of noise. Or was that the advice to scare away mountain lions? Rebecca couldn't recall.

The pots and pans that she and John banged with metal spoons as noisemakers to ring in every new year were on the other side of the door in the kitchen. The same kitchen the bear was looting right now. No doubt those very same pots and pans were being trashed by the bear at this very instant. Rebecca could feel her anger and courage growing with each successive crash echoing through her house.

Rebecca grabbed the only two noisemaking devices in the bedroom: her concert-size ukulele, a wonderful gift John had surprised her with last Christmas; and the ceremonial wooden recorder her brother had sent her from Papua New Guinea back when he was in college. Rebecca pulled both instruments off their display hooks on the wall and strode to the bedroom door. With one hand on the doorknob Rebecca turned to her dog stating, "Reni, let's do it."

"Mister Bear, I'm coming out of this room and *you* are getting out of my house," was Rebecca's battle cry in a volume and passion worthy of any warrior in any battle during any time in the history of Middle-earth.

Opening the bedroom door Rebecca couldn't see the bear, he was currently behind the kitchen island, but she could definitely hear him ripping something open. The refrigerator door was open with its contents strewn across the room and dog kibble seemed to be everywhere. The entire area looked like the floor beneath the stadium seats at AT&T Park after an extra inning game where the San Francisco Giants beat the Los Angeles Dodgers. The bear had ripped out a cupboard door to feast upon three bags filled with trash, recyclables, and vegetable compost. What really ticked Rebecca off was the sight of the handmade fruit bowl she had purchased from an artist at a street fair the summer she and John were married. Her favorite bowl was in pieces, and now she really lost control.

"Get your hairy butt out of my house!" she screamed, plucking the four ukulele strings harder than they had ever known. Alternating between banging the back of the ukulele with the recorder and blowing notes through the recorder that were in the key of piercing, Rebecca charged around the island confronting the munching bear. Rebecca kept up the yelling, plucking, banging, and blowing until the sounds had the desired effect. This bear was as interested in Rebecca's concert as Rebecca was interested in having him as a houseguest. He stopped his foraging and looked at Rebecca with his cracker covered nose which was answered by Rebecca's rapid fire plucking and yelling "Get out!"

Once Rebecca had the bear moving toward the open front door, she threw a few things at him too. Books, a cordless phone, two couch cushions, a jar of mayonnaise, and a remote control for the television, all bounced off a furry bear backside but did their job in herding the intruder out the door.

Slamming the door with a fist pump, Rebecca momentarily celebrated her victory and adrenaline spike with a few primal screams before falling to the floor in a heap of sweat and tears. Clutching her splintered recorder and her now two-stringed ukulele with a fresh hole in the side, she turned to take stock of her kitchen.

The place was thrashed. The broken fruit bowl was the biggest emotional loss, though John's comments later that evening about Rebecca's decision to throw the now useless television remote control at the bear came in a close second. John lost quite a few points in the thoughtful spouse category.

Wading into the lake of soy milk with islands of potato salad and plastic containers, Rebecca was fascinated by the bear's culinary tastes. The big tub of margarine and smaller tub of chocolate frosting were both licked clean, while the jar of natural peanut butter was open but hardly touched. All of the vegetables from the drawers were gone or at least partially gnawed, but the pickles and salad dressings were untouched. The squeeze bottle of ketchup was mangled, while the yellow mustard was intact. Leftover lasagna and a few bags of sliced turkey meat had been eaten and smeared across the floor, but a sourdough bread loaf and a jar of pesto lay undisturbed next to a pristine block of cream cheese. This was a discerning bear, perhaps with a lactose sensitivity similar to John's, as all of Rebecca's fancy smelly cheeses were left alone.

Surveying the damage, Rebecca realized she had been fortunate. The door to the cupboard beneath the sink would have to be replaced, but John could fix that. Food and trash were everywhere, but that could be cleaned. The refrigerator door worked, none of the shelves were broken, and only one of the vegetable drawers was damaged. The stainless steel refrigerator was supposed to have a "no fingerprint" finish, but paw prints and claw marks were clearly visible.

Rebecca sat on the floor next to a banana peel and grapefruit rind and made a few phone calls. She called 911 to report the bear, and they assured her Fish and Game would be right over. She called John to let him know what happened, and he now had a weekend project to replace a cupboard door. And she called the office to let them know that she'd had another "animal incident" and wouldn't be in today.

Reni walked into the kitchen and began lapping up the soy milk.

"I guess your bear chasing days are over," sighed Rebecca while patting her buddy on the head. "But you can still help me clean this up," and she set a partially eaten jar of peanut butter in front of her friend.

CHAPTER TWENTY-THREE

Big Dead Turkey Drive

If you're an out-of-towner visiting for the day, a new resident who has just arrived to our area, or if you're considering moving to the foothills, there are a few rules and expectations you should know about. Our new elementary school principal, Mitch Robinson, noted a few of these expectations as he took in the scenery during his long drive on his first day of work. Other rules Mr. Robinson would learn over time.

First, you're not really a local unless you have some mechanical parts sitting around on your property. The rules are pretty simple. If you live on a lot within the city limits, you should have a few tires or at least the bare wheels sitting in front of your garage. The tires or wheels may be inside the garage, but then you need to keep your garage door at least partially open. A nonfunctioning vehicle visible from the road is also nice, but not mandatory.

Property owners of one-half to one-acre lots should definitely have one nonfunctioning vehicle visible at all times, car or truck is permissible. You should also have an old lawn mower or other large power tool, that you plan to repair someday, visible for others to see. This tool may be in your garage, but once again you must keep your garage door at least partially open.

One to four-acre land owners have the option of two or more nonworking vehicles on the property or in place of the vehicles they may have a tractor, dump truck, or one of assorted large earthmovers such as a backhoe. In addition, these parcels shall have one seagoing storage container, preferably rusted, or the trailer end of a large diesel truck from a moving company or business that is no longer in operation. Either of these may be substituted with a train car, your choice of boxcar style. Special notice is given to those who have a caboose on their land. Possession of a functioning train whistle is considered trite and frowned upon, while having metal railroad and highway signs is just being social.

Larger scale properties of five-acres and up should have all the above plus evidence of an unfinished building project that utilized mechanical equipment. Acceptable examples include a large pit, foundation, or wall of some kind. Note: the evidence should show the project was initiated, but not completed.

As a local foothill resident you are also expected to house animals, both wild and domestic. Residents close to downtown should maintain the requisite pet dogs and cats. Both species can be helpful in protecting your person and property from encounters with wild creatures. Chickens are fine so long as you're willing to eat your rooster if the surrounding property owners complain about the noise, otherwise stick with hens. Fish and birds are allowed in your home, just don't talk about them much or you'll annoy your neighbors.

Once you pass the two-mile radius from the downtown area, your responsibility to own an unusual or exotic species increases at a rate corresponding to your distance from the Bell Tower on Main Street. Horses, cows, and llamas are commonplace while extra stars are awarded to landowners with bison, camels, or zebras. At the four-mile radius mark you can find a rhinoceros, but nobody is supposed to know about that one so don't spread it around. Emus are encouraged, as long as you're willing to show off the eggs and walk your emu down Main Street at least once a year.

Receiving your mail offers you some choices too. Sure, you can rent a post office box or your neighborhood can pool funds and buy one of those silver, metal, multi-box stands. The multi-box makes delivery easy on the postal worker, but you're missing out on an artistic opportunity of self-expression through mail box design. The basic red barn with white trim or bird house style is good for wood workers or those who like to build projects from kits. Older folks tend to go with wrought iron scroll work on their boxes, while earth lovers experiment with boxes made from recycled tires and plastic milk jugs. Gardeners often go with colorful flower designs, hippies run with tye-dye themes, and no-nonsense accountants set out the basic black box that says, "Just put the mail in the box."

While you're contemplating the design of your mailbox, you should also be thinking about naming your street, easement, or if it is long enough, your driveway. The city will tell you, "No, you can't do that," but once you put up the sign it's a done deal. Folks start using the name and pretty soon the post office falls right in line. Of course if your street already has a name or if you've got neighbors using the same road, changing the shared street name might not be such a bright idea. If you do put up a new sign, just make sure the local fire and law enforcement authorities know about the change if you expect to receive their assistance some day.

As for the actual name you choose for your road there are various approaches to this topic. Some folks go for the pastoral tone: Pleasant Drive, Forest View Road, Rolling Hills Way, Shady Glen Road, and Storybook Lane. Ornithologists have Blue Jay Way, Great Heron Drive, Hawk's Flight Court, and Oriole Lane even though the only orioles visible in this area are the ones you see on television from Baltimore that play against the New York Yankees. Animal lovers have Squirrel Hill Drive, Raccoon Trail, Cougar Trail, Grizzly Court, Coyote Ridge Trial, and Timber Wolf Drive, though you won't find a timber wolf within five hundred miles of here.

Water themes are popular with Grizzly Creek Road, French Creek Road, Cedar Creek Road, Perry Creek Drive, and Cold Creek Court among your choices. If you prefer springs over creeks you might like Cold Springs Road, Wentworth Springs Road, or Hidden Springs Road, if you can find it.

Some street names go for the more direct, utilitarian approach. In town you'll find Airport Road, School Street, Church Street, Sawmill Road, and don't forget Throwita Way which you drive on to get to the garbage dump. Historical references are common with Prospector's Trail, Gold Pan Way, Gold Hill Road, and Marshall Way, all paying tribute to James Marshall's discovery of gold in 1848.

The most interesting street names may be accurate descriptors of the area, but you shouldn't expect your property value to skyrocket if you live on Mosquito Road, Locust Avenue, Shoo Fly Road, Hard Luck Lane, Broken Gate Road, Rattlesnake Drive, or Poverty Hill Road. There are two schools of thought on the reasoning behind these particular names. First, is the notion that these names are just spot-on accurate as to what you'll find as you drive down the road. But the second idea here is that each of these areas is drop dead gorgeous, local residents don't want anyone to know about their little slice of heaven, and the name is really a strong attempt to keep out any land developers. You're free to draw your own conclusions, but if you take a drive out Slug Gulch Lane you'll want to claim a parcel and homestead the land before you get two minutes down the road.

Perhaps the most important rule and expectation of living in the foothills is the belief of helping out your neighbor. *It takes a village....We're all in this together....Treat others as you wish to be treated....Put your brother before yourself....Not unto ourselves alone are we born.* However you choose to phrase the concept, if you're going to live here you'll be a much happier and contented person if you put the idea into practice.

Mitch Robinson knew he'd made the right decision about taking this new job as principal on his very first day of work when he was the recipient of this practice.

Any job in education is a position of trust. Parents, children, the whole community have to trust those individuals in charge of teaching tomorrow's leaders. But the job of school principal brings another layer of trust and responsibility. Teachers and all school employees must see someone who they can count on in a crisis, who is a model of behavior, and who earns the respect of the staff. An experienced leader, Mitch was aware of this and wanted to make a great first impression on day one with his new staff.

Mitch planned to arrive at school two hours before his first staff meeting. That would give him plenty of time to arrange everything just the way he wanted to set the tone for the year: tables and chairs in a circle, supplies ready and waiting, and a nice selection of healthy snacks to keep everyone happy and engaged in the activities planned for the day.

Mitch had not moved to town yet. He lived down in the valley about an hour and half drive from work which meant waking up rather early for this first day. His drive to town was a pleasant one. Back roads winding through the hills were a more direct route than traveling out of his way to find a state highway. The path was also much more enjoyable without any oncoming traffic or glare from headlights in the morning darkness.

Mitch's brain was filled with excitement as he anticipated the day, checking off every item on his list that he'd accomplished and ready to complete those left unchecked. He listened to no music or morning news as he was happily focused on the day's events. The drive was uneventful for over an hour until Mitch rounded a curve and caught a momentary glimpse of a large black feathered object in his headlights which was immediately followed by a thump, crash, and spray of glass which glittered across the windshield of his nine-year-old, four-door, compact sedan.

Pulling over to the shoulder, Mitch got out to survey the situation. The headlight and cover were history, there was some body damage up front, and the bumper and grill would both need some attention. Nothing serious, but the damage would need to be dealt with. Looking around Mitch saw what he thought was the largest turkey on the planet, or at least part of what was once the largest turkey on the planet. Certainly a bigger bird than he'd ever seen on any Thanksgiving table. The sun was beginning to rise but Mitch still had plenty of time to get to work. "This is why you plan ahead and leave early," thought Mitch.

Which was a good thought until Mitch started up the car only to find it would not start. A second and third attempt were fruitless as well. Mitch Robinson has never been a mechanically inclined guy. So far in life he's been successful with the motto, "You don't teach your own kid, and I won't fix my own car." That outlook has served him well in a thirty-year career in education and a nine-year relationship with his vehicle, but Mitch is competent enough to lift a hood and look for the obvious.

In this case the obvious was the other part of what was once the largest turkey on the planet. Though Mitch is no chef or ornithologist, he was able to correctly identify a few assorted bird parts that were now residing in the engine compartment in front of him. "Hmmh," he sighed as he looked at the feathered mess.

As Mitch was contemplating arriving late or not arriving at all on his first day of work, a pair of high beams rounded the same curve where the planet's largest turkey had just met his end. The pickup pulled over beside Mitch with a voice calmly asking, "You need some help?"

"Yes, I guess so," answered Mitch.

"Watcha got here?" asked the man stepping down out of the cab.

"I hit the world's largest turkey," explained Mitch.

"You're not from around here, are ya?" asked the man who appeared to be about sixty.

"No, not yet. I'll be moving here soon though. I just got a new job. In fact, today is my first day. I'm the new principal at the school," said Mitch.

"Well Mr. Principal, here's your first lesson. You didn't hit the bird. He hit you," explained the man as he looked under the hood.

"Pardon me?" asked Mitch.

"Yep. The turkey hit you. It might a been a suicide. You know how depressed turkeys can get. You better learn that quick if you're gonna live up here," answered the man as he was tinkering with the engine.

"I've got to learn that turkeys are depressed?" asked Mitch.

"You're from the city aren't you?"

"Yes. Does it show?" replied Mitch.

"The animal always hits you, you never hit the animal. You better get that straight before you talk to your insurance agent," explained the man. "You're gonna need something a little tougher if you're gonna drive these roads. This little car can handle a skunk, squirrel, or even a chicken. But you're gonna have trouble with a raccoon or a coyote. And when a deer hits you, you're really gonna know about it."

"Really?"

"You need something bigger, a little higher off the ground," he advised as he came out from under the hood. "Well, I can't fix it here. Can I give you a lift to work?"

"You'll give me a ride to work?" replied Mitch.

"You know, you answer a lot of questions with another question. I guess that's an educator thing. Yes, I'll give you a ride. I got the space. You need a ride," replied the man. "Get your stuff and climb up."

As the two men drove the last twenty minutes to school the conversations were friendly, polite, and varied. No politics, but they did talk about the weather. No religion, but they spoke of family. No popular culture, but they did discuss fishing.

Turning on School Street and pulling up to the school parking lot, the man asked, "You want me to look at your car?"

"You'll look at my car?" asked Mitch.

"You're doing it again."

"Sorry," replied Mitch without a question.

"Yes, I'll look at your car if you give me your keys."

"You want my keys?" asked Mitch who quickly caught himself and added, "Yes. I'd appreciate you looking at my car very much." Mitch was now laughing at himself as he realized his city fears and recognized his car would be of no use to this man.

"I'll call you at the school and let you know what I find out."

"I never introduced myself," said Mitch stepping out of the truck. "I'm Mitch Robinson."

"Good to meet you Mitch. I'm Jackson Baxter. You'll be hearing from me," answered Jackson as he pulled away.

Later that afternoon as Mitch sat at his desk for the first time that day checking items off his list and smiling about how great the day had turned out, his secretary Margaret came in saying, "Jackson Baxter is here to see you."

Mitch stepped out of his office and warmly greeted Jackson with an outstretched hand which was met with a broken radiator hose and an electrical wire of some sort slapped in his palm.

"She's running again. Just a few things whacked out of place," explained Jackson.

"You fixed it already?" asked Mitch.

"You're gonna have to break that habit of yours Mitch," answered Jackson.

"What do I owe you for your time?" asked Mitch which he thought was a legitimate question.

"Just pay me for the parts is all," replied Jackson. "Welcome to town."

After just one month at his new job, school principal Mitch Robinson has purchased five-acres several miles north of town. "My wife and I love it here, so we're building a house," explained Mr. Robinson. "Construction should start in the spring, but the road to the building pad is already cut."

"My wife and I are having some trouble agreeing on a name for the road," added Mr. Robinson. "She likes Shady Oaks Trail, but I'm partial to Big Dead Turkey Drive."

Stay tuned.

CHAPTER TWENTY-FOUR

A Weekend with Walt

Walt Peterson had planned to spend the weekend checking off a few odd jobs on his self-imposed chore list, but by the time the weekend was over he had accomplished nothing except adding a few more chores to the list.

All week Walt was looking forward to Saturday morning which he had set aside to stain and waterproof the redwood patio cover that was attached to the back of his house. The structure was several years old and in good shape, but winter rains and summer sun had taken their toll. So Saturday was a great day to give all the wood a fresh coat of sealer. That is until his grandkids called inviting him for a quick trip to the coast for a day of body surfing in Santa Cruz. As any grandfather can tell you, it is difficult to say no to your grandkids and when you throw in bodysurfing? Walt was more than willing to trade sealing wood for catching waves.

The day at the beach with family was wonderful, everything you expect from a day with sun, sand, and surf. Standing on the beach, watching the grandkids curl their backs, and seeing them riding the waves into shore was a wonderful sight. And when Walt was in the water with the kids, side by side, riding the white-water wave crests, his vision was impeccable. This sight of bodysurfing with his grandchildren was so crisp in his mind he found himself overcome with joy. Walt could not recall a memory like this so clearly. Then he realized why this vision was so clear, but it was too late. As Walt reached up to his face, one falling whitecap crashed on his back ripping his glasses off his face.

A few pointless grabs at the seabed and Walt stood up on the shore. With waves lapping at his knees, he squinted up the beach. Walt heard Barb call out, "What's wrong? You look pained."

"You remember *The Incredible Mr. Limpet*? Well, I've just made some crustacean very happy."

Walt was working at a decent pace on Sunday morning, considering his impaired vision. Staining the patio cover did not require any distance vision and Walt didn't mind squinting while he worked. He figured it would just make him pay more attention to detail, so the patio cover would be the beneficiary of his goofball mistake made while bodysurfing. With no twenty-four-hour eye doctor in town, Walt would just have to wait til Monday to get some new specs. Walt is generally good at laughing at his klutziness, but this event did point out he should have replaced his backup pair of glasses after last summer's incident with the belt sander destroyed his old pair.

About an hour into the morning's project, Walt was happily sitting atop the structure staining the cross pieces when he was interrupted by Barb announcing that "Three guys in orange vests are at the door. They want you to flush some tablets down the toilet."

"What?"

"Maybe you should come speak with them."

The three guys were workers from the city investigating a sewage leak in the area just downhill a bit from Walt's place. They were trying to track down the source of the leak and did request that Walt flush five purple dye tablets down the toilet.

Then they would know if the leak was coming from Walt's plumbing. You don't generally see city employees working on Sunday, so Walt figured this was legitimate and agreed to flush the tablets. The men said they'd be back either way to let Walt know the result. If the trio noticed Walt squinting, they didn't mention it.

Walt went back to staining while Barb hopped in the shower to get ready for a baby shower she was attending with friends. Within fifteen minutes the group of orange-vested men was back, but this time there were four of them.

"Yep, it's your pipe. You're gonna have to fix this thing," announced the grungiest of the group.

"I have to fix it?" replied a stunned Walt.

"I'm afraid so sir. We've determined the sewer pipe is yours. Your pipe runs downhill from here, crosses several private properties, and doesn't enter the city sewer system until it joins it under the street," explained the newest and cleanest member of the group.

"And you're sure it's my pipe?"

"Yep, it's yours," answered the grungy guy again.

"Well you guys need to show me what you're talking about. How about you give me some more of those tablets, I come with you, and we get my wife to flush tablets?"

"Certainly sir," answered the new guy.

Walt filled Barb in on the plan and then explained to the work crew about his missing glasses so they'd have to take him down to see this pipe. The five of them loaded up in the city truck and drove down the hill.

"So I figure you got that sunburn at the beach?" asked the grungy guy.

"Pardon?" asked Walt.

"Your face is all red. You forgot to put on sun lotion."

"Yesterday wasn't one of my better days," answered Walt. "But at least some mackerel will have a better view of the sea."

Standing at the site, Walt was surprised to see the broken pipe was only a few inches below the surface. The city boys had exposed the damaged area between the creek bed and the side of the road explaining "Somebody probably drove off the side of the road and over the pipe one too many times. The pipe just wasn't deep enough to take the weight."

Not yet convinced this mess was his responsibility, Walt said, "Let me call my wife and have her flush the tablets," which Barb did immediately and then announced she was heading out to the baby shower.

"I can't see a thing," said a squinting Walt.

"Give it a minute or two sir. Water takes a while to run through several hundred feet of pipe," replied the new guy.

"I still can't see anything," said Walt getting down on his knees for a better view.

"It'll be here, don't you worry," announced the grungy guy.

"No, it's my eyes. I just can't focus," explained Walt who was now laying on the ground. "What if I get down low enough to see inside the..." which was a sentence interrupted by a gushing blast of debris-filled purple water hitting the right half of Walt's face.

A chorus of "Eww" from a group of grown men joined a spitting and sputtering Walt who headed straight to the creek bed to clean his face.

"I'm sorry about this sir, but you have to deal with this pipe. And with the creek so close, now that you have been notified of the leak, you've got twenty-four hours to clean it up before it gets reported to the state as an environmental hazard."

"Okay. I understand. I'll take care of it," answered a still spitting Walt standing in the creek. "Thanks guys."

"Take care sir," spoke the new guy, as the four men got in the truck and headed out to brighten someone else's day on a Sunday afternoon.

Walt didn't actually see them drive away, but as he heard the truck rattle down the street it occurred to him he couldn't see well enough to walk home. Walt's phone was in his left pocket so it was spared the purple moisture that now dominated the right side of his body. He thought about calling Barb to come pick him up, but she was so looking forward to this time with her friends Walt decided to call Rob Taylor instead.

Rob was happy to help and said he'd be there in less than twenty minutes. Waiting on the side of the road for less than five minutes, a half purple Walt was spoken to by a man in a car that had slowed to a stop beside him.

"What happened to you?' asked the man.

As Walt explained his coloring, he approached the car and soon realized he was speaking to a police officer.

"But you're only half purple, the other half is red?" asked the curious officer.

"Well, yes, the red was from yesterday," Walt continued with his explanation. He could tell the lawman enjoyed his story, particularly the Mr. Limpet part, because the officer took pity on him and offered him a ride home.

"You'll have to sit in the back though. You're a real mess."

"You can find your front door okay?"

"Yes. Thank you. I'll be fine," replied Walt with a wave of his hand as the blurry patrol car backed out of the driveway.

The front door was easy to find, but finding a way inside was now a challenge as Walt realized he was locked out of his own house. Barb was always conscientious about locking up the whole house whenever she left and Walt's keys were no doubt sitting on the nightstand next to his bed.

"Fine," thought Walt, "I'll go in through the slider upstairs." The upstairs deck was a small cafe style patio just off the master bedroom. A sliding glass door allowed access from the bedroom to the deck and would work just as well going the other direction. Walt smiled as he finally got to see a payoff from not finishing something on his chore list. The lock on the bedroom sliding glass door had been broken for years and the project never made it to the top of the list.

Getting on the roof to reach the upstairs patio wasn't a particularly difficult task. Walt had been on the roof countless times over the years, mostly to clear out the gutters of fallen oak leaves. Walt just needed to use a ladder to get on top of the redwood patio cover, then he could step right on to the roof. And the ladder was already set up under the patio cover from this morning's staining project.

Somewhere between being not a particularly difficult task and being on the roof countless times, combined with his being in the middle of a staining project and his lack of proper vision, Walt found he had a problem. As he was nearing the top of ladder, Walt was losing his balance. Whether it was from not seeing that he had set one leg of the ladder in a soft planter bed rather than on the firm concrete patio, or if it was from not seeing that he'd set up the ladder too far from the top beam of the patio cover to get a good grip, it really didn't matter. Walt was losing his balance and falling from the top of an eight-foot ladder. Instinctively he reached out and grabbed the first thing available to steady himself, which was the uncovered five-gallon bucket of waterproofing stain and sealer which had been left on top of the patio cover from this morning's work.

Stain flew everywhere: on Walt, his clothes, the ladder, the patio, and thankfully on a small mugo pine that helped cushion his fall. Of course Walt couldn't see how bad it was, but he knew he'd just added "staining the rest of the concrete patio so it matches" to his list of chores. With nothing much injured but his pride and a sore foot, Walt sat in his sticky mess, spitting out stain and wiping the liquid from his now stinging eyes.

"Need a hand?" asked Rob Taylor walking into the backyard. "I couldn't find you, so I thought maybe you tried to walk home."

"The cops gave me a ride up the hill. Help me up here, would you?"

"Not until we clean you up a bit. Let me grab the hose."

Walt rinsed his eyes first and then let the cold water run over what was left of his hair. "One of the few advantages of going bald," explained Walt, "It's easier to get stuff off your head."

"You get a lot of stuff on your head, do you?" deadpanned Rob.

"On occasion. Now would you help me up?"

Which was easier said than done. As soon as Walt put weight on his right foot he nearly crumbled back down to the freshly stained patio.

"Damn. I think it's broken."

"Maybe it's just a bad sprain. Take your shoe off and I'll take a look."

"No, trust me, if I take off the shoe it will swell like a balloon. Better to just leave it on," professed Walt.

"You speak from experience?" asked Rob.

"Yeah, well, would you take me to the emergency room?"

"Sure. At least let me go inside and get you some ice first."

After Walt explained to Rob why that wasn't possible and what he was doing climbing the patio cover to begin with, Rob helped the hobbling Walt out to his car.

"Mind if I put you in the back? You're kind of a mess."

"I just appreciate the ride," answered Walt, as he leaned in through the back hatch of Rob's old Volvo.

"You want me to call Barb? She's at that baby shower with Jen."

"No, let her have some fun," answered Walt.

"Maybe on the way you can explain to me why you're purple and red when you're working with a brown stain."

"Hey Walt. What's up?" Walt couldn't see her, but he recognized the emergency room admitting nurse's friendly voice.

"Hi Maria. Little trouble with my ankle here. I think it's broken."

"What did you do Walt?" asked Maria.

"Fell off a ladder, reached out to keep my balance, and dumped a bucket of waterproof stain on my head."

"Hmm. Okay, so that would explain the brown. Why is half your face and shirt purple?"

"That was an earlier accident. Unrelated."

"And does the sunburn fit into any of this?"

"That's when I decided to give my glasses to a fish."

"On a scale of one to ten what is your pain?" asked Maria.

"Only a two right now, but it's growing. When the adrenaline rush wears off, I'd say we're looking at a four."

"Any of your information change?" asked Maria typing.

"No."

"You want me to call Barb?" said Maria.

"No thanks. She's at a party." replied Walt.

"Sounds like you guys have done this before," commented Rob impressed with the flow of information.

"Once or twice," answered Walt who couldn't see Maria's huge smile and nodding head.

"I'll call Jen and Barb and let them know where we are," said Rob.

"Thanks Rob," replied Walt waiting for a wheelchair to take him to an exam room.

After a few minutes Rob joined Walt in the exam room reporting, "I just spoke with Jen. Barb's at the party with a washcloth on her head. Something about a dead body at the baby shower and Barb asking a lot of questions. Jen said don't worry, everything is fine. She's taking Barb home."

CHAPTER TWENTY-FIVE

The Baby Shower

Shortly after Samantha Thompson's wedding memorial, which you should really go back and read if you haven't already, the forty-five-year-old *not to be* bride sent out invitations to a baby shower. Baby showers are not uncommon after weddings, but rarely do the showers occur after wedding memorials where a wedding never actually took place.

This baby announcement raised a lot of eyebrows around town. A few pious folks didn't care for the whole single mother idea, while others thought that forty-five was a bit old to begin a family and bring a baby into the world. Those who knew Samantha best weren't concerned about either of those issues, but they were curious about how Samantha would handle the demands of a newborn while running her thriving landscaping business and maintaining her ever-growing rabbit, ferret, and sad animal farm at home.

All of these concerns were somewhat baseless because Samantha was not pregnant. Samantha was adopting. Looking to cheer herself up after her non-marriage to Dr. Michael Smith, Samantha decided to fill the hole in her life by adopting....wait for it, a dog.

Yes, Samantha was adopting a dog. One of those small annoying dogs that some women like to carry in their purse. The kind of dog that continually shakes and looks scared to death all the time. The kind of dog owners of large dogs refer to as a "two bite dog" as in their large dog could consume this smaller dog in two bites. The kind of dog most self-respecting dog owners refuse to accept as a dog. Samantha was adopting a Chihuahua. And Samantha was throwing herself a baby shower to celebrate the new addition to her family.

The invitations were blue, but the theme was pink. Which made sense since the dog was a male, but would be raised as a female. The golden brown Chihuahua named Roxie, in honor of Sam's love of rocks, would be officially welcomed to the Thompson family on a Sunday afternoon.

After planning to attend a wedding dressed in Halloween attire, but really ending up sitting through a memorial service, followed by dancing in an apple orchard to the "Monster Mash" you could understand some people's reluctance to attend Samantha's baby shower for a dog. Perhaps out of curiosity for the event, recognition of the strife Samantha had been through, or just kindness and excitement for a friend, a dozen ladies arrived to celebrate Roxie's arrival.

Pink balloons, each with a painted paw print larger than a Chihuahua's head, graced the doorway welcoming twelve brave women. Samantha greeted each guest with a warm right arm hug being careful to showcase and not crush Roxie, who was safely tucked in her pink wicker basket cradled in Samantha's left arm. Her love of music and themes not to be wasted, Samantha's home was filled with pink balloons, crepe paper streamers, and the soft sounds of Donny Osmond singing "Puppy Love."

The pink party atmosphere was almost strong enough to overcome the aroma of Samantha's other house guests. Almost. Her four ferrets were corralled in the guest room behind a baby gate installed in the doorway. Apparently Roxie was nervous around ferrets. Currently the indoor privileges for Samantha's indoor-outdoor rabbits were also under review as Roxie was nervous around rabbits as well. But Roxie didn't have any issues with cats, as Bob, the cat with no eyelids rescued from a university lab down in the valley, was still allowed full access to anywhere in the house.

"What do you bring to a baby shower for a dog?" is a question easily answered in today's world thanks to the internet. Pink personalized dog collars, bowls, and beds are all available at the click of a button and were greatly appreciated by an excited new parent who "oohed" and "awed" at the unwrapping of each thoughtful gift. Homemade dog biscuits were a treat as was the pink knit dog sweater with the cowl neck which Samantha noted "perfectly accented the brown and pink of Roxie's ears."

The big hit of the gathering was the dog ramp. Jennifer Taylor knew Roxie would be too small for your average dog stairs, so she made a customized dog ramp, complete with low pile, pink carpeting, enabling Roxie to climb up to any couch or bed that Samantha desired. With Van Morrison's "Brown Eyed Girl" playing in the background, Samantha enticed Roxie up the ramp to a waiting biscuit, homemade and held by a smiling Barb Peterson sitting on the couch. Rebecca Forrester chuckled unnoticed as she realized the golden brown Roxie climbing the ramp looked like a walking Twinkie with ears. Rebecca's stifled laughter was due to both the visual of the dog and the realization she hadn't thought of Twinkies since an attack of the munchies during her freshman year of college.

A pink frosted, red velvet layer cake, shaped and frosted somewhat like a Chihuahua, which when cut gave the unfortunate appearance of a dog undergoing an autopsy, was surprisingly tasty. Although everyone noted that perhaps the next time someone ordered a custom cake shaped like an animal it might be best to leave out the red filling between the two layers.

The visual of the cake prompted Samantha to talk about how helpful Roxie would be in her new second job. Samantha explained that in addition to running her landscaping business she was now, for the past month, a Mortuary Assistant. That new information was greeted with dead silence by all the ladies in the room, but didn't stop Samantha from continuing with her story.

"When someone, generally an elderly person, dies at home, and there are no suspicious circumstances the local mortuary is called to collect the body and transport it back to the mortuary." Enter Samantha Thompson.

"You have to be strong enough to lift the body onto the stretcher," said the lady who moved rocks and drove a backhoe for a living.

"You also have to be good with people," explained the woman who never advertised because all of her landscaping jobs were found by referrals from satisfied customers who were now friends.

"And you need to have a compassionate heart," said the soul who saves rabbits in her spare time.

"Sometimes the family members want to talk for a while or they just need a hug," continued Samantha. "Roxie will be perfect for people to cuddle and pet while I'm taking the body out. They can talk to her or just hold her close. I think this will really help with the grieving process."

The twelve shower attendees still hadn't said a word, so Samantha continued. "Once I put the body in the van, Roxie can ride in her basket up front with me. I don't do the embalming so Roxie won't have to worry about that. I'll put her new bed in the workroom. She can stay there and keep me company while I use the cremator."

"You cremate people?" uttered Barb, which was the first response from the group.

"Well of course. Someone has to do it. I'm not allowed to embalm the deceased. We call them the deceased, not stiffs, by

215

the way. But I get to put them in the refrigeration units and I run the cremator. Then I have a lot of paperwork to do. You'd be surprised how many forms you have to fill out when someone dies."

"I can't imagine," answered Jennifer.

"The mortuary, county, and state, all have forms to fill out. Sometimes the family wants us to scatter the ashes for them which means even more forms."

"And Roxie can be in there with you?" asked a wide-eyed Barb.

"Sure. It takes at least two hours to cremate someone, sometimes longer, so Roxie can keep me company."

"Does it really take two hours?" asked a now pale faced Barb.

"At least two hours. It depends."

"On?" asked Barb who later wondered why she'd asked.

"How big the deceased is. The cremator is really hot, but bigger bodies take more time. And if the family wants the ashes returned to them that takes a longer time too."

"Because?" asked Barb who now realized she couldn't seem to stop asking questions that she didn't want answered.

"If the family gets the remains, you want the ashes to be much finer than if we're scattering them. Oh, and the magnet takes a little time to use too."

"You use a magnet?" asked Barb who was now being poked by Jennifer in an attempt to stop this conversation.

"You know, I think there's one more gift left to open," interrupted Jennifer standing up. "Let's see what else Roxie has to play with."

While Jennifer redirected the baby shower back to approved baby shower activities, Rebecca escorted Barb to the kitchen for a glass of water and a cool dish towel for her forehead. "I don't know. I just couldn't stop," Barb tried to explain while leaning over the kitchen sink.

As is the case in most gatherings, after awhile the large group broke into several smaller conversations about various topics. Understandably most of the topics began with dogs. When Rebecca caught sight of two of the ferrets attempting to scale the baby gate and perhaps make a break for a piece of the remaining cake, she noticed the ferrets had a slight unfortunate resemblance to rats.

Now anyone living in the foothills has experience with rats. Like it or not, rats are a common occurrence right along with deer, skunks, and raccoons. All these creatures are pests that foothill residents have to deal with, but the rat suffers from a particular image problem that Bambi, Flower, and Rocky do not.

Rebecca learned that lesson the hard way several years ago while at a party in a rather posh neighborhood in San Francisco. Rebecca's sister had invited her to a gathering at a friend's house and while answering questions about "how nice it must be to live so close to nature in the foothills" Rebecca had told one of her rat stories. Not a particularly gross or detailed recounting, just an explanation of how the rats had found their way into the air duct system under the house and were happily breeding in the warmth provided by central heating. From the immediate shunning Rebecca received as a backwater bayou resident who couldn't keep her home clean, she learned how important it is to assess your audience before telling a rat story. Stick with the Bambi stories when you're in the big city.

In this setting Rebecca knew she was safely among her fellow foothill warriors who occasionally go into battle with Mother Nature. So when she saw the ferrets fruitlessly trying to climb the baby gate, Rebecca remembered the day she, John, and their dog Reni had cornered several rats in a woodpile under the deck in their backyard. As Rebecca explained how the three of them worked as a team on opposite sides of the pile using shovels, booted feet, and Reni's jaws to take down three of the rats, her friends laughed and smiled while listening to the adventure. When Rebecca started dancing, explaining how a fourth rat scooted out of the pile, ran right between Reni's feet, and found refuge in a scrap piece of drainpipe near a shed, that's when Samantha heard the words "rat" and "dog" in the same sentence.

Although Samantha was speaking with Barb about dog biscuit recipes, her newly acquired protective motherly instincts kicked in.

"Roxie does not look like a rat," barked Samantha.

"No, Samantha, I wasn't talking about Roxie. I was watching your ferrets and they made me think of..."

"My ferrets are not rats either," interrupted Samantha.

"I didn't mean to imply..." Rebecca attempted.

"Roxie is not a rat. She's a beautiful, short hair Chihuahua. I can't believe you'd insult my dog like this. And during my baby shower."

"Samantha, I'm sorry. I wasn't talking about..."

"My dog may be small, but at least I don't electrocute my animals. You and your husband should be..."

Fortunately for Rebecca, Samantha's increasing volume was cut off by Jennifer answering the home phone, "Samantha, you have a phone call. It's Dr. Michael Smith." Which seemed like a good moment for the baby shower to end.

Rebecca knew she would eventually smooth things out with Samantha, but it's doubtful Samantha Thompson will be doing any landscaping work at the Forrester's place for a while. And if Rebecca or John pass away unexpectedly in the next few weeks and Sam is the one who picks up the deceased, the surviving spouse will most likely have to cope without the compassionate services of Roxie the Chihuahua.

Several residents on the north side of town have reported encounters with an overly friendly deer this week. "He's a big one," explained John Forrester. "I don't know if he's sick or injured, but I walked out my front door and there he was standing on the porch. He looked like he wanted some food or a beer. I walked toward him and then he went over and stood next to my car, like he wanted a ride somewhere. Then he just kind of wandered off down the hill."

Locals are reminded not to feed or encourage deer to stay on your property.

CHAPTER TWENTY-SIX

The View from the Swings

Tino and Lisa De Luca received another unofficial welcome to the foothills this week. The De Lucas are the Italian family that moved into town a while back and have been warmly welcomed by just about everyone. During their first year adjusting to life outside the big city, they've learned many lessons about life in the country, but this particular lesson turned out rather messy. If you're squeamish about cleaning the Thanksgiving turkey you might just want to hop over this story, but if you enjoy your steak grilled with some color still in the meat, you'll be just fine.

Lisa took Friday off work to run some errands and hang out with her two boys, Michael and Rocco, in the park for the afternoon. As any wise parent with a six and four-year-old will explain, you always do the errands first and finish your outing with the fun stuff. As the three De Lucas walked out the front door across the elevated front porch deck, they noticed an unusual smell wafting through the area. Definitely not a skunk, but the odor certainly had an animal quality of some measure.

"Hmm. That's a new smell boys," said Mom.

"It stinks," stated Michael.

"It's unpleasant. Come on, it'll blow away," replied Mom.

The family loaded up in the vehicle and headed out for their day together. A short stop at the Post Office to mail a package, a longer stop at the shoe store to find sneakers for all three of them, and a much longer stop at the clothing store to find some pants and shirts for two rapidly growing boys. That was followed by a tour of the grocery store which included picking up some snacks to nibble on while at the final stop of the afternoon, the park.

Two happy boys attacked the slides, tunnels, rocking horses, sand boxes, and grassy fields. The big draw of the park is the swings. As Michael says, "I want to go the pom swings." The "pom" Michael refers to is actually "The Swing" a poem by Robert Louis Stevenson which is inscribed on a plaque above the swings.

> *How do you like to go up in a swing,*
> *Up in the air so blue?*
> *Oh, I do think it the pleasantest thing*
> *Ever a child can do!*
>
> *Up in the air and over the wall,*
> *Til I can see so wide,*
> *River and trees and cattle and all*
> *Over the countryside--*
>
> *Til I look down on the garden green,*
> *Down on the roof so brown--*
> *Up in the air I go flying again,*
> *Up in the air and down!*

Lisa reads the poem aloud to the boys while they pump and pull for the sky. The boys have never seen cattle when they reach the top of each pump, but they have seen a fox and plenty of deer. And so each time they ride their pom swings they watch and hope to spy a animal roaming the surrounding hills. Michael was disappointed with today's viewing saying, "I only saw part of a deer this time. He was standing behind a tree."

After swinging, time is spent running, chasing, and climbing which is followed by the usual tripping, falling, and crying. In a little over an hour the flow of tears reached any parent's saturation point and Lisa knew it was time to head for home.

Being away from the house for a little more than four hours was just enough time to allow the afternoon summer sun to really warm the place. Pulling in to the driveway Lisa thought the afternoon heat might be just enough to entice the boys to pick a few blackberries from the bushes at the lower portion of their sloped two-acres before curling up for a nice afternoon nap in the lounge chairs on the front deck.

But when the De Lucas climbed out the car they were swamped by a nauseous wave of putrid something. Whatever the smell was, it had not blown away. Four hours of afternoon sun was just enough time and heat to ferment whatever was cooking.

"Mom!" cried Michael.

"Hold your nose," commanded Mom.

"Mommy!" cried Rocco.

"I can taste it in my mouth!" yelled Michael.

"Then hold your breath until we get inside," ordered Mom. "I'm calling your Dad."

When Tino arrived home and stepped inside the house his first words, "Whoa! You're not kidding. What the heck is that?" were greeted with "I don't know, but you're getting rid of it."

Based on Lisa's tone, Tino began his investigation without delay and quickly found the source of the smell beneath the deck right under the front door to the house.

"It's a deer," Tino reported back inside the house, "and he's really bloated."

"Spare me the details. I don't want to hear about it. It's not staying under my front door. The smell is in the house. Just get rid of it. Get rid of it now."

When Lisa speaks Tino listens, but when Lisa speaks in short sentences with a clenched jaw and determined eyes Tino listens intently. So Tino immediately called Animal Control where a friendly female voice told him yes they will pick the deer up, but not until Monday morning at eight o'clock. She politely explained that it was ten to five on a Friday and there was no one around to take the call.

"So what am I supposed to do? This thing really stinks!" asked Tino.

"You could put some lime on it," answered Animal Control.

"What does lime do?"

This question was followed by a crash course in the usage and benefits of lime in such situations. The cheerful lady even offered a few suggestions where Tino could purchase bags of lime.

Tino shared the disappointing news with Lisa who wasn't interested in learning about lime, where you can buy lime, and what lime does to the carcass. She just wanted the smell gone. "Move the deer Tino. Get it as far away from the house as you can." Tino understood this was not a request.

Tino went back down beneath the deck stating, "It's me and you bud." Receiving no response, Tino grabbed the deer's rear legs and began to pull. Getting a good grip and really using his muscles, Tino successfully moved the buck somewhere between one and three inches. He also made the mistake of holding his breath while grunting and exerting himself, followed by deeply exhaling when he let go. Which meant deeply inhaling to replenish his body's oxygen supply, which completely filled his lungs with the pungent odor of the bloated buck.

After a few gasps along with some spitting, Tino retreated to the house for a pair of work gloves and a wet bandana to cover his nose and mouth. The boys spotted their costumed Dad and thought this was an invitation to play bank robber which was denied by Mom.

"I can still smell it Tino," stated Lisa.

With nose, mouth, and hands now protected Tino went back for round two replying, "This is going to be harder than I thought."

Now if Tino had asked for help, any one of his friends or neighbors would have come to his aide, but for Tino this was man versus beast. This was the former denizen of the city conquering the frontier country. So you can feel sorry for Tino for what happened next, but remember, he did this to himself.

As Tino began his second attempt at pulling out the deer, the buck's antlers got hooked up in one of the beams supporting the deck and the extra deer fencing that he had stashed under the deck. The coincidence of fencing used to keep deer out of the garden that was now keeping a deer under the deck was not lost on Tino. Even after he got the deer out from under the deck, the antlers would still be a hinderance. Tino realized moving the buck to the farthest point away from the house to the lower part of the property would be much easier if the antlers were gone.

We'll skip some of the details here, but for future reference Tino discovered a standard hack saw cuts through deer antlers just fine, but an electric reciprocating saw is much quicker and better suited for the task.

Bringing a power tool to the situation opened Tino's eyes to new possibilities. Why drag a three hundred pound buck by hand when you could hook it up to the back of your riding lawn mower? Rewetting his bandana Tino gathered enough ropes and bungee cords to lasso the buck's legs and pull him out from under the deck. Taking the first turn gently, Tino headed around the house and down the slope dragging his prize behind him at a motorized pace slower than your average window shopper. He was feeling rather proud and even imagined himself a real cowboy having just roped a calf in a rodeo, right up until the buck's bloated belly caught on a rock and popped releasing a toxic cloud that penetrated right through his cowboy bandana.

After a time out for some fresh air, Tino remounted his steed and continued his slow journey, dragging the buck down the hill to the edge of their two-acre property. Lisa would be pleased; this was as far as he could get the deer away from the house.

Somehow a man always feels more like a man when power tools are involved and Tino was no different. He was pumped when he unhooked the buck from the back of the mower. He realized the job took him three hours, but if this is what it takes to protect your family when you live in the country, so be it. Looking back up the pathway Tino saw he'd left a distinct red trail with some pretty gooey stuff spread out along the way. A little clean up was necessary as he retraced his path with a flathead shovel and a bucket to remove the assorted debris that fell out of the deer during the trek from the house.

"Can't have those boys playing with deer guts," stated Tino as he finished the clean up.

Monday morning at eight o'clock a big guy in a truck from Animal Control showed up right on time. Tino was pleased that this man was so huge. No doubt the officer could sling this buck over his shoulders, carry him up the hill, and catch a stray dog at the same time.

"Where is it?" the officer asked.

"Come on down here. I'll show you," answered Tino. "I'm glad to see you. This thing is a real stinker. I had to..."

"Sir, didn't they tell you?" interrupted the officer.

"Tell me what?" asked Tino.

"I'm not allowed to go on to private property to collect an animal. You have to place the carcass on the side of the road."

"What? No, it's okay. It's my property. You can come on..."

"I'm sorry sir."

"No, really. It's fine. I'm inviting you on my property," tried Tino.

"I can't..." the officer attempted to explain.

"You don't understand. It took me three hours to drag the thing down hill. You've got to take it with you," pleaded Tino.

"You put the deer down there?"

"Yes, it really stinks. I had to get it away from the house," answered Tino.

"I'm sorry sir. Do you want me to come back another time?"

A deflated and dejected Tino answered, "Eight o'clock tomorrow morning work for you?"

"I'll be here," responded the officer.

The three hours spent dragging the buck's body down the hill was easily matched bringing the carcass back up the hill and placing it on the side of the road. Tino discovered a dead deer dragged uphill doesn't travel nearly as well as a dead deer dragged downhill. With the punctured belly and the body fermenting over the weekend, the deer's joints had stiffened up a bit. After the rear leg with the rope attached detached itself from the rest of the body, Tino momentarily thought of the reciprocating saw again. Smaller pieces would be easier to move, the job could get done quicker. But Tino realized as much as he enjoyed horror films he could never go through with the deed. Cutting antlers was reasonable, but he wasn't cut out to butcher a buck.

While daydreaming about *The Silence of the Lambs*, Tino did think about wrapping the buck in a plastic tarp. Using a tarp wouldn't change the overall weight, but the tarp would make the carcass easier to pull and slide up the hill. Plus, the problem of additional deer parts ripping off would be solved.

Late Monday afternoon all four De Lucas hopped in the car for a well-deserved trip to the park. As they pulled out of the driveway Lisa distracted the boys pointing out some birds in the blackberry bushes on the right side of the car. Tino stared to his left at the blue plastic tarp concealing a lump of deer parts awaiting their pick up on Tuesday morning.

"Who feels like doing some swinging?" asked a proud Dad.

"Me!" chimed two boys in unison.

"And I hope we get to see a whole deer this time," added Michael. "Last time I only got to see part."

Police were called to the north side of town Monday night to investigate a report of a possible dead body. A passerby phoned in a call about a body wrapped in a blue tarp on the side of the road. Blood stains were allegedly visible.

Responding officers found a dead deer inside the tarp. "He was pretty messed up. We thought we might have some bizarre cult activity on our hands," stated Officer Bercelli. "But a nearby property owner explained the situation. Everything is fine."

Animal Control has been notified.

CHAPTER TWENTY-SEVEN

The Bench and the Bell Tower

A few topics of discussion have been brewing around town lately. Naturally our City Council, which is known for making rash decisions and occasionally overreacting, jumped right in the middle of all of them.

A bench in front of the Downtown Clothing Company on Main Street was the origin of the first debate. Debi and Dale, owners of the shop, decided to place a redwood bench on the sidewalk in front of their store. An attractive, comfortable bench meant for resting your bones for a bit while shopping downtown. Park yourself on their bench and you've got a fine view of the Bell Tower and both ends of Main Street. A good place to people watch while you catch your breath.

The trouble began with what was along the back side of the six-foot-long bench, a raised planter box. Flower beds Debi had filled with rich potting soil, the kind with the white granules that hold in the moisture, and a few dozen bright yellow marigolds. Late one night some local chowderhead pulled out the plants and made quite a mess scattering flowers and tracking soil all over the north side of Main Street. Debi and Dale cleaned up the mess when they arrived at work the next morning, but apparently not quickly enough to satisfy everyone in town. Somebody complained to Council Member Dr. Marcus Gilbert about the mess and the campaign to ban benches on Main Street was underway.

After Dr. Gilbert lodged his initial complaint at the council meeting, Mayor Carl Romano joined in detailing the complaints he had received about skateboarders using Debi's bench, and a few others, as an obstacle course. Youth roll down the sidewalk and as the board approaches a bench "the kid leaps up and attempts to land on the board as it comes out the other side," explained Carl.

Charlie Tuttle, the council's elder statesman and owner of several downtown properties and businesses, shared he'd been receiving comments about loitering around the benches and the Bell Tower (but we'll stick with the benches right now and get to the Bell Tower later). He suggested "Removing the benches would solve both the loitering and the skateboarding problems at the same time."

Carl Snyder, an insurance salesman and the council's other Carl, was really bothered by the skateboarders jumping over the benches wondering aloud "What kind of liability position do those benches put the city in? What if one of those kids gets hurt on city property? And we don't need folks sitting around on Main Street anyway. We want them in the shops."

So on a night when Council Member Deborah Singerman was home sick in bed with a nasty stomach bug, she no doubt picked up from one of her first grade students, the council voted 4-0 to instruct city staff to remove all the benches on Main Street.

Now when Charlie mentioned the Bell Tower, that opened up another can of worms for the council to tackle. Apparently, unbeknownst to most of us in town, our Bell Tower has become a hot bed of criminal activity.

The structure of the Bell Tower looks innocent enough. About three stories tall, constructed of thin metal girders, the tower is more reminiscent of one of those lonely electrical towers used to string power lines across a barren plain hours away from the nearest gas station. No one is going to confuse our Bell Tower for the Eiffel Tower, but this is our Bell Tower and we like our landmark all the same.

A twenty-foot by twenty-foot square concrete patio is beneath the tower creating a gazebo with a shingled roof covering most of the floor space. Four soon to be removed benches sit on the concrete protected from the hot summer sun and occasional winter snows. Up at the top of the tower is another shingled roof, this one just large enough to protect the town bell that rings on the hour starting at 8:00 am and ceasing at 9:00 p.m. And if you're guessing the council had a few thoughts on determining those bell ringing hours you'd be correct.

The Bell Tower is located right smack in the middle of downtown. The main flow of traffic is on the south side, but you can drive your car all the way around the tower. Any downtown pedestrian can cross the street and walk around the structure on the patio that's raised above the street level by a foot.

In addition, the Bell Tower gets dressed up for special occasions, turning into a beer stein for the annual Brewfest, a hypodermic needle and vial for a blood drive, and a giant firecracker complete with sparklers and bunting every Fourth of July.

Dr. Marcus Gilbert, often referred to as the "How did this guy get elected?" council member, explained the alleged criminal activity included loitering by local youth. Dr. Gilbert charged that he often sees kids hanging out under the tower. "I can't hear what they're saying, but I can tell they're up to no good."

Carl Snyder complained he was tired of seeing families jaywalking just so they could take some photographs of the tower. He wondered "What kind of liability position does this put the city in? What if someone gets hit by a car while they're jaywalking to reach the Bell Tower?" And of course those benches just encouraged more people. The Bell Tower just attracted too much attention, and perhaps they should be talking about removing the whole tower not just the benches.

Charlie Tuttle shared a story about finding some french fries on the Bell Tower's patio while he was sitting there eating his lunch last week. Mayor Romano added he found the melted remains of half an ice cream cone on the patio when he and his wife were having their traditional Sunday afternoon coffee and apple fritter under the Bell Tower just last week.

So on the same night when Council Member Deborah Singerman was home sick, the council voted 4-0 to implement a new city ordinance with a set of ten rules to be posted at the base of the Bell Tower.

Bell Tower Rules

1. No climbing on the Bell Tower.

2. No eating on the patio area.

3. No loitering.

4. No photography.

5. No skateboards.

6. No more than two people at a time may stand under the tower.

7.

8.

9.

10.

Rules 7-10 were left blank because the council knew there should be more rules about the Bell Tower, but it was getting late and everyone was tired. City staff was directed to implement the new ordinance, notify the police department, and get working on the sign tomorrow.

An emergency meeting of the City Council was held last night after an angry group of senior citizens complained about the removal of all the benches on Main Street. "We've got no place to sit," complained Mary Thorpe. "Where am I supposed to wait for the bus?" demanded an irritated Max Brown.

Council Member Deborah Singerman apologized for the council, explaining that all the benches will be replaced, even those under the Bell Tower. Mrs. Singerman further commented that the council voted 5-0 to place aesthetically pleasing trash cans shaped liked whiskey barrels along Main Street at appropriate intervals. And a new crosswalk will be painted on Main Street to allow safer access to the Bell Tower and patio. Mrs. Singerman also announced that City Ordinance 32110.4 regarding Bell Tower Rules had been rescinded for further review.

City residents are reminded that council elections are in two months, but interested parties should register to vote at least one month ahead of time.

CHAPTER TWENTY-EIGHT

There are No Dogs at Mostly Franks

When Frank and his wife Sally divorced about forty years ago, Frank couldn't afford to buy out her half of Frank and Sally's, the bar and barbecue rib place they owned together on the south side of town for the previous fifteen years. What Frank could afford was to buy out 10% of Sally's share which would make him the majority owner in charge of all decisions and Sally a silent, unlike their marriage, partner. Frank's first official act as boss was to change the name from Frank and Sally's to Mostly Franks. The motivation here was primarily just to irritate Sally, but the new name was an accurate reflection of ownership.

After just two years of majority rule, Frank died in an unfortunate accident involving a large keg of beer and some neighborhood cats. Mostly Franks immediately closed and Sally, through the power of Frank's procrastination regarding a change in his will, found herself the sole owner of a bar and restaurant she wanted nothing to do with.

Sally quickly sold the place to some low-life character who had little class and less business sense. Mostly Franks reopened and soon degenerated into the type of joint you only frequented if you were looking for trouble. With the volume of traffic coming in and out of the old cut stone and brick building with no windows, most folks in town suspected the business had become home to a drug czar or was run by the mob. The truth was if a drug czar or the mob had run the place, the interior and exterior would have been in better shape. The owner was into various illegal activities, but he wasn't very good at any of them.

Local police busted his customers on a regular basis and the business was shut down several times due to various investigations. Finally the feds showed up and closed the place down for good. Mostly Franks sat sad and vacant for over a year.

Which brings us to eight years ago when Jesus Martinez bought the building and wisely decided to keep the name Mostly Franks. Jesus's Place did not have the same sound and he wasn't looking for business on a Sunday morning anyway. Jesus briefly considered Hey Zeus for the phonetic spelling, but figured no one else but him would get the joke. If he was going for total accuracy, the place should be named Mostly Wells Fargo's, at least for the next twenty years. Ultimately the decision came down to finances. The cost of replacing or fixing the two-sided neon sign buzzing Mostly Franks above the front door was just too high for a new business to undertake. So was the notion of replacing any of the cracked leather bar stools, patched red naugahyde booths, or broken linoleum floor tiles. Mostly Franks was reopened as a cleaner version of itself.

Jesus was using the original Frank's recipes for the ribs, he hadn't changed anything inside or out, and at five-foot eight-inches tall, two hundred fifteen pounds Jesus looked more like a Frank than a Jesus anyway. Regardless of how many times he introduced himself as Jesus Martinez, folks called him Frank, so eventually Jesus just accepted his new name. Over time Frank came to appreciate his dual identity and business name with one exception. The missing apostrophe. Frank knew the name should read Mostly Frank's as in Mostly Frank's Place. The missing apostrophe led to at least one customer a day coming in and making a hot dog joke. Eight years of daily hot dog and wiener jokes is asking a lot of anyone, but Frank smiles as best he can.

Business was good for Frank. He never advertised, but developed a following and reputation for great food and strong drinks at a fair price. Mostly Franks was the hole-in-the-wall kind of place that enough locals and out of town customers knew about to keep business humming along nicely. Frank knew he would never be rich, but so long as he kept his customers and the neighborhood happy he would lead a good life.

Keeping the neighborhood happy meant never getting too loud on a Friday or Saturday night. So Frank was a little apprehensive about scheduling and reserving space for two separate gatherings last Saturday night. He agreed to both parties, a birthday party and a bachelorette party, because they each began at six and would be finished up by eight or nine when the place really got busy.

The birthday party was a surprise gathering to celebrate John Forrester's 50th birthday. Rebecca Forrester had been planning this party for her husband for over a month. She'd invited friends, neighbors, and most of her staff at the real estate office to meet in the parking lot at Mostly Franks at six o'clock on Saturday night. In a moment of weakness Rebecca agreed to accept the help of John's buddy and fellow teacher Barry Reese in spreading the word about the party. Barry was in charge of inviting the staff at school to come to the party. No gifts, be on time, and don't tell John.

According to plan, Rebecca called John at five o'clock explaining she was still showing a house but didn't want to lose their reservation, so John should go ahead and she would meet him there. John did as he was told and entered Mostly Franks at six to grab a booth and wait for his lovely wife.

Walking inside, John immediately saw several women from work surrounding the bubbly Samantha Thompson. Before John had a chance to sit down or say hello he was warmly welcomed, "John, it's so good of you to come. Can you believe I'm getting married? Rebecca mentioned you two had another commitment and couldn't make it tonight, but I'm so glad you're here." Which was followed by an affectionate bear hug.

"We wouldn't miss this," answered John who knew the benefits of staying on the good side of Samantha Thompson.

Being the only guy at Samantha's bachelorette party wasn't awkward for John as he was accustomed to being surrounded by women at work. He and Barry were the only men at school and it had been that way for quite a few years.

Meanwhile outside in the parking lot, Rebecca arrived expecting to meet up with fifty people to walk in and surprise John. She found Rob and Jennifer Taylor, Walt and Barb Peterson, Tino and Lisa De Luca, and most of her office staff waiting for her, but no Barry and no one at all from John's work.

Hoping to buy a few more minutes, Rebecca phoned John explaining she'd be there in ten minutes. John's end of the call was noisy and Rebecca didn't understand his response of "Have I got a surprise for you!"

Rebecca phoned Barry but he didn't answer his phone. "He probably left the darn thing somewhere," muttered Rebecca.

"Let's not wait any more," announced Rebecca. "Let's go surprise John and get this party started."

As the group passed the bouncer in the doorway, Rebecca spotted John in a group of women at the bar, "There he is! Come on!"

With the cheer of "Surprise!" coming from the Taylors, Petersons, De Lucas, a few real estate agents, and a glowing Rebecca, John turned around to face his wife and was not so gently knocked aside by the outstretched arms and voice of Samantha Thompson saying, "Oh Thank you! Can you believe I'm getting married?"

"No," mumbled Walt low enough so no one heard except Barb who elbowed her husband in the gut.

Samantha hugged everyone, but a stunned Rebecca received the longest embrace. "I'm so glad you came. This means so much to me," said Samantha as both women exchanged forgiveness for the rat misunderstanding of earlier days.

"I told you you'd be surprised," smiled John as he kissed his wife hello.

Appetizers at the bar, beer from the tap, and plenty of ribs, slaw, and bread filled the rest of the evening. Happy friends, good conversations, and even a little dancing, which made Frank nervous since he wasn't permitted for dancing, filled the building. Rebecca quietly arranged for the "Happy Birthday" icing to be wiped off the sheet cake and replaced with "You're Getting Married!" spelled out with beer nuts.

As eight o'clock neared Rebecca's group headed for the exit, said goodnight to the bouncer, and stood out front of Mostly Franks debriefing the events of the last two hours. Their chatting was interrupted by the panicked sounds of someone running down the alley alongside the building. A call of "Help!" had the entire group step around the corner into the alley where they were face to face with a surprised friend.

"Barry?" said everyone. "Are you okay?"

"I was being chased by cats," answered Barry catching his breath and setting down four large brown bags balanced on top of two large cardboard boxes. "What are you guys doing here?"

"We just came from a bachelorette party for Samantha Thompson. Big crowd. Great ribs. Lots of folks you know. What are you doing here?" answered John.

"I ordered ribs for fifty people. I thought I was on the way to your house for an eight o'clock birthday party...and I'm going to be a little late," explained Barry.

"You're a lot late Barry. The party was at six o'clock and it was here. Not at our house," growled Rebecca.

"Wait, I just had a birthday party?" asked John.

"Well, the people I invited are coming to your house at eight to celebrate John's birthday with some ribs. It's about eight now, so we should get going. They're probably wondering where we are," said Barry.

"Happy Birthday honey. You up for another rib dinner?" asked Rebecca.

"Mostly Franks, best ribs in town!" answered John.

As the troops headed out to their vehicles for the trek over to the Forrester's, no one seemed to notice the four large brown bags balanced on top of two large cardboard boxes leaning against the old cut stone and brick building at the edge of the alley.

Later that night as the fifty guests at John Forrester's second surprise 50th birthday party munched on delivered pizza, a contented group of joyfully satisfied alley cats could be heard purring, "Mostly Franks, best ribs in town."

About the Author

Kristopher Schultz is a middle-aged, married guy with two daughters in college. He's also been a public school teacher for twenty-seven years. Kris is known to carry both antacid tablets and lactose intolerance pills in his pockets at all times, though he claims neither has anything to do with his family or career.

www.facebook.com/kristopherschultzauthor

www.kristopherschultz.com

Made in the USA
Lexington, KY
23 June 2013